AROUND TOWN
For the Elliotts, does history repeat itself?

Magazine mogul Daniel Elliott has been seen around town squiring none other than his ex-wife, Manhattan defense attorney Amanda Elliott.

The pair was spotted locking lips in New York's "hottest" eatery one night, then at a black-tie charity ball. In a designer original, the free-spirited, quirky Ms. Elliott looked stunning, though she only had eyes for her dashing ex. Together the couple have two sons, Bryan Elliott, owner of the fabulously successful uptown restaurant Une Nuit, and Cullen Elliott, his father's protégé at *Snap* magazine. To all in eyeshot, however, the couple seemed interested in more than their children....

Neither Daniel nor Amanda Elliott was available for comment, but the attorney's secretary did speak to reporters, claiming there was "nothing going on" between her boss and her ex, whom she called "Mr. Delectable." No argument here!

Whatever is going on must be something spicy. According to sources at Elliott Publication Holdings, workaholic Daniel has been missing from his corner office of late.

Can't help but wonder, though, what that curmudgeon, patriarch Patrick Elliott, will have to say about this "family reunion"!

D1011805

Dear Reader,

Like Amanda Elliott, I married my high school sweetheart. He was two years older than me and had a really great car. Although we never got divorced—in fact we just celebrated our twenty-fifth anniversary—like Amanda and Daniel, we've been through many changes in our lives. I met a race car driver with a passion for noise and acceleration. I ended up married to an outdoorsman who dragged me up mountains and across rivers.

It was pure delight to write about the relationship between Amanda and Daniel. I admired their passion, the strength of their convictions and their finely honed ability to tease the heck out of each other. There's nothing like jokes to keep you on your toes.

I hope you enjoy *Marriage Terms,* and I'd love to hear from you! You can e-mail me through my Web site, www.barbaradunlop.com

Happy reading!

Barbara Dunlop

BARBARA DUNLOP

Marriage Terms

Published by Silhouette Books
America's Publisher of Contemporary Romance

For my sisters. Denise, Karen and Melinda

Special thanks and acknowledgment are given
to Barbara Dunlop for her contribution to
THE ELLIOTTS miniseries.

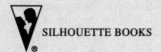

SILHOUETTE BOOKS

ISBN-13: 978-0-373-76741-0
ISBN-10:   0-373-76741-2

MARRIAGE TERMS

Copyright © 2006 by Harlequin Books S.A.

This edition published by arrangement with Harlequin Books S.A.

Visit Silhouette Books at www.eHarlequin.com

Printed in U.S.A.

Books by Barbara Dunlop

Silhouette Desire

Thunderbolt over Texas #1704
Marriage Terms #1741

BARBARA DUNLOP

writes romantic stories while curled up in a log cabin in Canada's far north, where bears outnumber people and it snows six months of the year. Fortunately, she has a brawny husband and two teenage children to haul firewood and clear the driveway while she sips cocoa and muses about her upcoming chapters. Barbara loves to hear from readers. You can contact her through her Web site at www.barbaradunlop.com.

THE ELLIOTTS

Patrick m Maeve O'Grady

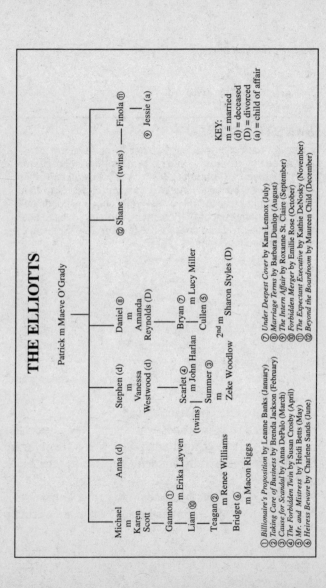

KEY:
m = married
(d) = deceased
(D) = divorced
(a) = child of affair

① *Billionaire's Proposition* by Leanne Banks (January)
② *Taking Care of Business* by Brenda Jackson (February)
③ *Cause for Scandal* by Anna DePalo (March)
④ *The Forbidden Twin* by Susan Crosby (April)
⑤ *Mr. and Mistress* by Heidi Betts (May)
⑥ *Heiress Beware* by Charlene Sands (June)
⑦ *Under Deepest Cover* by Kara Lennox (July)
⑧ *Marriage Terms* by Barbara Dunlop (August)
⑨ *The Intern Affair* by Roxanne St. Claire (September)
⑩ *Forbidden Merger* by Emilie Rose (October)
⑪ *The Expectant Executive* by Kathie DeNosky (November)
⑫ *Beyond the Boardroom* by Maureen Child (December)

One

If Amanda Elliott had her way, New York would have a law against ex-husbands. She took a deep breath, curled her toes over the pool deck at Boca Royce Health Club and dived headfirst into the fast lane.

A law against ex-husbands who invaded a woman's life. She stretched her arms out, surging her body forward until she sliced back up through the surface.

A law against ex-husbands who stayed fit and sexy for over fifteen years. Her right arm pulled into a freestyle arc as she kicked into her rhythm, letting the cool water block out the world.

And a law against ex-husbands who held a woman tight, whispered words of comfort and made her insane world tip right again.

She scrunched her eyes shut against the illicit memory, stroking hard until her fingertips brushed the smooth pool wall at the opposite end. Then she twisted her body to kick into the next lap.

While the politicians were at it, they should write a law against sons who were wounded in shoot-outs, sons who were secretly government agents and sons who went to spy school *without* their mother's permission.

It wouldn't take much. A simple amendment to the admissions disclaimer, and no woman would ever again have to wake up and discover she'd given birth to James Bond.

Amanda pulled past the blue halfway floats.

Her son Bryan was James Bond.

She laughed a little desperately at that one, nearly sucking in a lungful of water.

Try as she might, she couldn't imagine Bryan with a forged passport, driving exotic cars through foreign countries and pressing little remote control devices to blow things up. Her Bryan loved puppies and finger painting, he lived for those sweet little cream-filled coconut puffs you could only get at Wong's on the corner.

She was grateful he was getting out of the spy game. He'd vowed as much to his new bride. Amanda had heard it with her own ears. So had Daniel.

Her stroke faltered. This time her ex-husband's image refused to disappear.

Daniel had comforted her through the long night of Bryan's surgery. He'd been her pillar of strength, holding her up when she swore the sheer weight of terror would topple her. At times, he'd squeezed her so tight that over a decade and a half of anger and mistrust melted between them.

Détente?

She made another turn, pushing off the pool wall with her feet and knifing back to the surface. She swam harder, and her jaw tightened as she concentrated on her strokes.

Détente wasn't even a possibility.

It would never be a possibility.

Because Daniel was a true-blue Elliott. And Amanda...wasn't. East-West relations were a cakewalk compared to that.

The truce was over. Bryan was well on the road to recovery. Daniel was back on his own side of Manhattan. And Amanda had opening arguments in front of Judge Mercer tomorrow morning.

Her knuckles hit the wall at the end of another lap. *Five,* she counted off in her mind.

"Hello, Amanda." Daniel's familiar voice came out of nowhere.

She scrambled to bring her body to vertical, scrubbing the chlorinated water out of her eyes and blinking at her ex-husband's fuzzy image. What was he doing here? "Is it Bryan?"

Daniel flinched, quickly shaking his head. "No. No. Sorry. Bryan's fine." He crouched on the concrete deck, putting them closer to eye level.

Amanda whooshed out a breath of relief, clinging to the trough at the edge of the pool. "Thank goodness."

"Cullen told me I'd find you here," he said.

Her anxiety rushed back at the mention of her second son. "Is it Misty?"

Another shake of Daniel's head. "Misty's good. The baby's kicking up a storm."

Amanda studied his expression. His face was calm and impassive. Whatever had dragged him out of the office in the middle of the day wasn't life threatening.

He straightened back to full height, and her gaze strayed to his muscular chest, then to his navy trunks. His feet were bare, and he sported a six-pack of a stomach that would be the envy of a man half his age.

Her mouth went dry, and she suddenly realized she hadn't seen Daniel in anything but a designer suit for sixteen years. The man who had hugged her goodbye had a body to die for.

She bicycled her legs, trying to restore her equilibrium in the deep water. "Then what are you doing here?"

"I'm looking for you."

She blinked again, trying to make sense out of his words. Unless she'd missed something, they'd said their goodbyes at Bryan's wedding and had gone back to their respective lives.

Daniel should be perched behind his mahogany desk at *Snap* magazine right now, fighting tooth and nail with his siblings over profits and market share. As he was locked in a battle for the CEO position at Elliott Publication Holdings, it should have taken a catastrophe of biblical proportions to get him out of the office during work hours.

"I wanted to talk to you," he said casually.

"Excuse me?" She shook the water out of her ears.

"Talk. You know, when people use words to exchange information and ideas."

Clearing her ears hadn't helped. Daniel had tracked her down to *chat?*

He smiled, bending at the waist to reach out his hand. "Why don't we get a drink?"

She pushed away from the pool edge and began treading water. "I don't think so."

"Come out of the pool, Amanda."

"Uh-uh." She wasn't chatting, and she sure wasn't hopping out in front of him in a tight one-piece.

He might look like an advertisement for *Muscle Mass Monthly,* but the earth's gravitational pull was winning the war with her body.

"I've got forty-five laps to go," she said.

Fifty laps was a stretch, but she was upping her workout— starting here and now. Whether Daniel ever saw her in a bathing suit or not, a woman had her pride.

Daniel crossed his arms over his broad chest. "Since when do *you* stick to a plan?"

He wanted to start in on their weaknesses?

"Since when do *you* finish work before eight at night?" she asked.

"I'm taking a coffee break."

"Right," she drawled, with a skeptical nod.

He frowned, looking imperious despite the swimming trunks. "What's that supposed to mean?"

"It means you don't take coffee breaks."

"We've barely seen each other in over fifteen years. How would you know whether or not I take coffee breaks?"

"When was the last time you took one?"

His cobalt eyes darkened. "Today."

"Before that?"

He was silent for a moment, until one corner of his mouth quirked in a grin.

She splashed at him. "Knew it."

He ducked. "Do I have to come in there after you?"

"Go away." She had a workout to finish and a head to get clear. It was all well and good to lean on Daniel when their son was in mortal danger. But the truce was over. It was time to return to their respective trenches.

"I want to talk to you," he called.

She kicked farther into the lane. "We have nothing to say to each other."

"Amanda."

"If Bryan's not back in the hospital, and if Misty's not in labor, then you and I are leading separate lives."

"Amanda," he repeated a little bit louder.

"It says so on our divorce papers." She swam away.

He paced along the edge of the pool, his voice muffled by the water covering her ears. "I thought…then you…making progress…"

She gave up and turned into a sidestroke, gazing at his long, lean body while a shriek sounded from the diving pool. It was followed by the thump, thump, thump of the board's recoil.

"Progress toward what?"

His eyes narrowed. "I hate it when you play dumb."

"And I hate it when you insult me."

"How am I insulting you?"

"You called me dumb."

He spread his hands in frustration. "I said you were *playing* dumb."

"Then you called me scheming."

"Do we have to do this?"

Apparently, they did. Every single time they got within fifty feet of each other.

"I was there for you, Amanda."

She stilled, and the water lapped lightly against her neck. He was using it against her already?

He raised his palms in a gesture of surrender. "And you were there for me. I know. I know."

"And it's over," she said. "Bryan's alive…" Her voice cracked over her son's name, and she drew a bracing breath. "And Cullen is happily married."

Daniel crouched again, lowering his voice. "What about you, Amanda?" His blue irises flickered with the reflection of the water.

Nope. She wasn't doing this to herself. She wasn't getting into a conversation with Daniel about her emotional or mental state.

"I'm definitely alive," she informed him tartly, then did a surface dive and resumed her swim.

He continued walking along the deck, keeping pace, watching her strokes.

Soon, all she could think about was how far her butt was

sticking out of the water and whether or not her suit was riding up.

She paused at the opposite end, swiping her hair away from her eyes.

"Will you be leaving now?" she asked. She wasn't about to attempt forty-four laps with him sizing up her thighs.

"I want to talk to you about a legal matter," he said.

"Call my office."

"We're family."

She whooshed away from the edge, creating an eddy around her body. "We're *not* family." Not anymore.

He glanced around. "Do we have to do this here?"

"Hey, you can be wherever you want. I was swimming away, minding my own business."

He nodded toward the mezzanine floor that overlooked the pool. "Come up and have a drink."

"Go away."

"I need your legal advice."

"You have lawyers on retainer."

"But this is confidential."

"I've got laps left to swim."

His eyes focused on her blurred shape beneath the water. "You don't need them."

Her heart tripped over a beat. But then she remembered the way glib compliments rolled off his tongue. She turned and stretched into freestyle again.

He followed her to the other end and was standing there when she came up for air.

She sighed in frustration. "You can be a real jerk, you know that?"

"Go ahead and finish. I'll wait."

She gritted her teeth. "I don't think so."

He grinned and reached out his hand.

* * *

Daniel was worried she wouldn't fall for his ruse. Then he'd have to find another way to lure her into conversation. Because he definitely had a few things left to say.

Over the past few weeks, he'd seen her frantic schedule. He'd overheard the late-night calls. And he'd watched the way her clients took advantage of her.

Her dark eyes narrowed warily, and he moved his hand a little closer, wiggling his fingers in encouragement. He just needed her attention for a few days, maybe a couple of weeks. Then she'd be back on track, and he'd get out of her life for good.

Finally, she grimaced and tucked her small, slick hand in his palm. He tried not to be too obvious about his sigh of relief as he gently lifted her from the water.

She straightened on the deck, and he took in her toned limbs and the way her apricot suit clung to her ripe curves. Because she favored casual clothes now—clothes that tended toward loose and baggy—he'd thought maybe she'd gained weight over the years. Not so.

She had a ton of fashion potential. Her figure was gorgeous. Her waist was indented, her stomach smooth and tight, her full breasts rounded against the wet Lycra.

A long-dormant jolt of desire hit his system. He clenched his jaw to tamp it down.

If he alienated her now, she'd bolt. Then she'd spend the rest of her life swimming away her office hours and wandering around midtown Manhattan in khakis, gauzy blouses and clunky sandals.

He cringed at the image.

She might not admit it, but she needed to broaden her professional circles, cultivate prosperous clients and, for the love of God, dress for success.

She extracted her hand from his.

"One drink," she warned, giving him a don't-mess-with-me look as she whisked water droplets from her suit.

"One drink," he agreed gruffly, dragging his gaze from her luscious figure.

She took in his dry trunks, wrinkling her nose. "You didn't even get wet."

He cupped her elbow and turned her toward the locker rooms. "That's because I wasn't here to swim."

Her skin was slick and cool, like the tile under his feet. She stopped at the head of the corridor and turned to face him. He could almost see her mind ticking through the situation, formulating arguments.

He scrambled for a distraction. "Don't suppose you'd consider a family changing room for old times' sake?"

That put a flash in her mocha eyes, but it also shut her up. Which was what he'd had in mind.

He didn't really have a legal matter to discuss. It was a spur-of-the-moment excuse to get her out of the pool, and it was going to take a few minutes to put the finer points on the lie.

He gave her what he hoped was a nostalgic smile. "The boys sure loved it here."

"What is wrong with you?" she asked.

"I'm just saying—"

"Fine. Okay. The boys loved it here."

She was silent for a moment, then her eyes softened. He felt himself sinking into his own memories.

The shouts of children faded, and he suddenly saw two small, dark-haired boys whizzing down the slide and doing flips off the diving board. Boca Royce was the only recreation he and Amanda could afford during their lean years—thanks to the Elliott family lifetime membership. And Bryan and Cullen used to swim their little hearts out.

His memory moved on to the end of the swim day, when the boys were ready to drop. He and Amanda would bundle them home for frozen pizza and a cartoon movie. Then they'd tuck them in and curl up in their own bed for a leisurely evening of love.

His voice turned husky. "We had some good times, didn't we?"

She didn't engage, didn't meet his eyes. Without a word, she turned on her heel and marched down the corridor.

Just as well.

He was here to offer her a few basic pointers, to get her professional life on track.

Anything else was off-limits.

Way off-limits.

Amanda felt considerably less vulnerable in faded jeans and a powder-blue tank top. In the ladies' change room, she finger-combed her damp hair and smeared some clear lip gloss across her mouth. She never used much makeup during the day, and she wasn't about to put any on for Daniel. She wasn't blow-drying her hair, either.

Throwing her bright yellow athletic bag over one shoulder, she exited the change room and trotted up the wide stairs to the mezzanine.

One quick drink. She'd hear him out, refer him to somebody much higher priced than she was then maybe go see a good therapist.

At the top of the stairs, a set of arched, oak doors led to the pool lounge. A receptionist at the marble counter stopped her and asked to see her membership card. Before she could retrieve it from the depths of the bag, Daniel appeared, impeccably dressed in an Armani suit.

He took her arm and gave the receptionist a curt nod. "That won't be necessary. She's my guest."

"Technically, I'm not your guest," Amanda pointed out as he pushed on the oversize door. "I'm a member, too."

"I hate it when they card you," said Daniel, gesturing to a small, round table near the glass wall overlooking the pool. "It's so tacky."

"They don't recognize me," she said. The receptionist was only doing her job.

Daniel pulled out one of the curved-back chairs, and Amanda sat down on the leather cushion, plunking her bag on the hardwood floor.

"Maybe if you were to—"

She glanced at him over her shoulder.

He snapped his jaw shut and rounded the table.

As he sat down, a waiter in a dark suit appeared. "Can I get you a beverage, sir?"

Daniel raised his eyebrows in Amanda's direction. "Fruit juice," she requested.

"We have an orange-mango blend," said the waiter.

"Sounds good."

"And for you, sir?"

"Glen Saanich on the rocks. Yellow label."

"Very good." The waiter gave a sharp nod and left.

"Let me guess," she said, not in the mood to let the cut off insult slide by. "You were going to say that if I wore a power suit nobody would check my ID."

He didn't even bother to disagree. "The clothes do make the woman," he said.

"The *woman* makes the woman," she replied.

"A business suit and a nice pair of heels would give you a lot of credibility."

"I dress like that for the courtroom, not to get into exclusive clubs."

Daniel scooped the fanned, linen napkin from his water goblet and plunked it on the table. His study of her became more intense. "What *do* you plan your wardrobe around?"

"My life. My job. Just like everybody else."

"You're a lawyer."

"I'm aware of that."

"Amanda, lawyers usually—"

"Daniel," she warned. Whatever it was they were here to discuss, it wasn't going to include her clothing.

"All I'm saying is drop by a boutique. Get a standing appointment at a salon—"

"My hair?"

He paused and something flickered in his expression. "You're a beautiful woman, Amanda."

"Right," she huffed. Too bad she had ugly clothes and bad hair.

"I'm talking a couple of blazers and a bit of a trim."

"So I won't get carded at Boca Royce?"

"It's not just the ID card, and you know it."

She stiffened her spine. Maybe not. But it was also none of his business. "Back off, Daniel."

Unexpectedly, he held up his hands in surrender. A few beats later he offered an apologetic grin.

Somehow his easy capitulation felt unsatisfying. Which was silly.

He reached across the table and snagged her napkin, dropping it beside her glass so their view of each other was unobstructed. Her gaze caught on his strong, tanned fingers, and she had a split-second flashback to his hand against her skin. She swallowed.

Their waiter appeared, setting their drinks down on coasters and leaving an appetizer menu behind.

"Hungry?" asked Daniel, letting the menu fall open.

As if she was going to drag this out over phyllo or sushi. "No."

"We could get some canapés."

She shook her head.

"Okay. Then I'm good with the scotch."

She focused on the expensive amber liquid, ruthlessly reminding herself of who he'd become. It had been a long time since she'd served him Bud in a can.

"Thirty-dollar scotch?" she asked.

He closed the menu and set it aside. "What's wrong with the scotch?"

"You ever drink beer anymore?"

He shrugged. "Sometimes."

"I mean domestic."

He lifted his glass and the ice cubes clinked against the fine crystal. "You're a reverse snob, you know that?"

"And you're a straight-up snob."

He stared at her for a long moment, those knowing eyes sending a shiver up her spine.

Out of self-preservation, she dropped her gaze to the tabletop. She wouldn't let Daniel's opinion get the better of her. Forget the haircut. Forget the designer clothes.

His opinion of her meant nothing, nothing at all.

"Why do you suppose…?" he asked softly, and she glanced up. He started again. "Why do you suppose we argue so much?" The question was undeniably intimate.

She refused to match his tone. "Because we cling to the hope that one day we might change each other's minds."

He was silent for a long moment. And then a genuine grin grew on his face. "Well, I'm open to improvement if you are."

Uh-oh. She didn't know where he was going with this disarming act, but it couldn't be good. "Can we cut to the chase?"

"There's a chase?"

"The confidential legal matter? The thing you brought me up here to discuss?"

A fleeting expression tightened his features, and he shifted in his chair. "Oh, that. It's a matter of some, uh, delicacy."

That got her attention. *"Really?"*

"Yes."

She leaned forward. Was there a veiled message in those words? Was Daniel in some kind of trouble?

"You telling me you *did* something?" she asked.

He blinked. "Did something?"

"You actually broke the law?"

His brows knit together. "Don't be absurd. Jeez, Amanda."

"Well, then, what's with this secret meeting in the middle of the day? And why with me?"

"This isn't a secret meeting."

"We're not at your office."

"Would you come to my office?"

"No."

"There you go."

"Daniel."

"What?"

"Get to the point."

Their waiter appeared. "Anything from the menu, sir?"

Daniel barely turned his head. "The canapé tray will be fine."

"Very good, sir."

As the waiter left, Amanda raised her eyebrows in a question.

"You never know," said Daniel. "We might be here awhile."

"At the rate you're talking, we sure will."

He took a sip of his scotch. "Fine. I'll cut to the chase. I'm looking into an interpretation of our employee manual."

"The employee manual?"

How on earth was that a delicate matter? Here she thought the conversation, his life, was about to get interesting.

He nodded.

She shook her head in disappointment and reached for her athletic bag. "Daniel, I don't practice corporate law."

He trapped her hand on the table, and her entire arm buzzed with the sensation.

"What do you mean?" he asked.

She tried to ignore his touch. "I mean it's not my specialty."

"Well, maybe not labor relations…"

She shifted in her chair. She couldn't yank her hand from his. That would be too obvious. "I practice criminal law."

He stared at her in silence, the pulse in his thumb synchronizing with hers.

"Crime," she offered helpfully, tugging her hand ever so slightly.

He blinked in confusion.

"Surely you've read the newspapers, seen the dramas on television…"

"But… Private lawyers don't prosecute criminals."

"Who says I prosecute them?"

His hand tightened convulsively. "You *defend* them?"

"Yes, I do." She made no bones about trying to free herself this time.

He let her go. He glanced away. Then he stared at her again. "What kind of criminals?"

"The kind that get caught."

"Don't be facetious."

"I'm dead serious. The ones that get away with it don't need me."

"Like thieves, prostitutes, murderers?"

"Yes."

"Do the boys know about this?"

"Of course."

He hardened his jaw. "I don't like the sound of that."

"Really?" As if his opinion had any bearing on her career decisions.

"Really, Amanda." He reached for her hand with both of his this time. "I thought…" He shook his head. "But this is dangerous."

His touch might be disturbing, but his words were even more so.

She fought him on both fronts. "This is none of your business, Daniel."

He stared at her intently. "But it *is* my business."

"No."

"You're the mother of my children."

"No."

"I can't let anything—"

"Daniel!"

His hands tightened, and he got a familiar look in his eyes. That look said he had a plan. That look said he had a mission. That look said he was going to save her from herself.

Two

Daniel needed to talk to his sons. Well, one son, to start off with. He supposed he'd have to wait until the bandages came off to confront Bryan. But Cullen was getting a piece of his mind right away.

He tossed his credit card on the counter at the Atlantic Golf Course pro shop.

Amanda a criminal defense attorney? Of all the lunatic ideas. After their divorce she'd pursued her B.A., then a graduate degree in English literature, then three years of law school, and she was throwing it all away on lost causes?

The pro shop clerk bagged a royal-blue golf shirt, while Daniel signed the receipt.

Her clients probably paid her off in stolen stereos.

Maybe the bank robbers had cash—small, unmarked bills. And then only as long as they'd pulled a few successful jobs before they got caught.

His ex-wife was defending bank robbers. His sons had

known she was in danger. All these years, and they hadn't bothered saying anything. Was it not a salient point to bring up in conversation?

"By the way, Dad. You might be interested to know that Mom's consorting with thieves and murderers."

Sure, he and Amanda had agreed not to bad-mouth each other in front of their kids. And, for the most part, that meant not talking about each other in the early years of the divorce. But Bryan and Cullen were grown men now. And they were perfectly capable of seeing danger when it hovered in front of their eyes.

Daniel exited the pro shop and headed for the locker room. Misty had said Cullen's tee time was six-thirty. That meant he'd be coming up on the ninth hole about now.

At his locker, Daniel hung up his suit jacket, his tie and his dress shirt. Then he tugged the new golf shirt over his head and straightened the collar. He left the clubhouse through the terrace café.

Normally he'd check out the dining room, maybe exchange an informal word with some of his business associates. But not today. Today he marched straight down the shade-patterned pathway.

Cullen had some explaining to do.

Five minutes down the path, he spotted Cullen on the ninth green, lining up for a putt. He turned and angled toward him, not caring in the least about etiquette.

"Hey, Dad." A hushed voice to his left stopped him in his tracks.

He turned to see his older son. "Bryan?"

Standing at the edge of the green, Bryan sported a sling to protect his injured shoulder.

He nodded to Daniel.

"What the hell are you doing here?" Daniel hissed.

"I'm golfing," said Bryan.

"You're injured."

Cullen looked up from the putt. "Will you two shut up?"

Daniel clamped his jaw until Cullen's ball had disappeared into the hole.

"Hey, Dad," said Cullen, sliding the handle of his putter through his fist as he paced toward them. He handed the club to his caddy.

"You just got out of the hospital," Daniel said to Bryan.

Bryan headed for his own golf bag. "It was a superficial wound."

"It was a bullet hole."

"In my shoulder."

"You were in surgery for three hours."

Bryan shrugged his good shoulder and accepted a putter. "You know those doctors. They eke out every billable minute."

Daniel rounded on Cullen. "You actually brought him golfing?"

"I'm taking the drives," said Cullen easily. "He's only putting."

"And he's cheating," said Bryan, lining up his one-handed shot.

"Like I need to cheat to beat a cripple," Cullen called.

"I can't believe Lucy let you out of the house," said Daniel. Bryan had always been the daredevil of the family, but this was ridiculous.

"You kidding?" asked Cullen. "Lucy paid me to get him out of the house."

"Apparently I'm not a good patient," Bryan said, swinging at the ball and missing the hole.

"That's five," said Cullen.

"Yeah, yeah," Bryan returned. "I'll get you next week."

"Next week we're skydiving," said Cullen.

"I do not want to hear this," said Daniel, hoping against hope that it was a joke.

Bryan finally sank the golf ball. "Relax, Dad. It's an easy jump."

"I knew we should have resorted to corporal punishment," said Daniel.

Cullen laughed. "Where are your clubs, Dad?"

Daniel squared his shoulders. His sons might be grown men, and he might not have control over their hobbies, but he was still their father. "I'm not here to golf."

Bryan returned the putter to his caddy. "Yeah?"

"And I wasn't at Boca Royce to swim this afternoon, either."

After a silent pause, Cullen raised an eyebrow. "Uh, thanks for sharing that with us, Dad."

He pasted each of his sons with a significant glare. "I was there to talk to your mother." Then he dropped his tone an octave, giving his voice that steely undercurrent he'd used when they were teenagers and got caught drinking beer or breaking curfew. "She told me about her law practice."

He paused and waited for their reaction.

Cullen glanced at Bryan, and Bryan shrugged.

"Her *defense attorney* practice," Daniel elaborated, trying to crack their poker faces.

Bryan turned to leave the green. "Is something wrong, Dad?"

"Yeah, I'd say something was wrong. Your mother is working for *criminals*."

Cullen followed his brother, cocking his head to one side. "Who'd you think she was working for?"

Daniel stalked through the rough. "Executives, politicians, little old ladies writing wills."

"She's a litigator," said Bryan. "Always has been."

"And you never mentioned it?"

Cullen peeled off his white leather gloves and tucked them in his back pocket. "We don't talk to you about Mom."

"Well, maybe you should have."

"Why?"

Daniel couldn't believe his sons would be so obtuse. "Because, she's in danger, that's why."

"Danger from what?" asked Bryan.

"Criminals."

"She's not in danger," Bryan scoffed as they turned onto the pathway that led up to the clubhouse.

Daniel squinted at his older son. He sounded very confident, very definitive. And Bryan was in the business of danger.

Wait a minute.

Maybe he knew something Daniel didn't. That was it. Daniel should have realized he could count on his sons.

He felt as if a weight had risen right up off him. "Are you having her watched by one of your associates?"

Cullen sputtered out a laugh, while Bryan stared at Daniel. "Dad, you've seen one too many cop shows."

Daniel rocked back. They were mocking him now. "Her clients are thieves and murderers."

"And she's their best friend," said Bryan. "Trust me on this, Dad. The mortality rate for defense lawyers is pretty damn low."

"Are you two going to help me or not?"

"Help you do what?" asked Cullen.

Daniel's original plan was to work on her image and her business. But if he found a good clothing designer, it would only attract a better class of criminals. Nope. This called for drastic action.

"Convince her to change careers," he said.

His sons drew back simultaneously. Cullen actually held up crossed fingers as if to ward off an evil spirit.

"Uh-uh," said Bryan with a shake of his dark head.

"Are you out of your mind?" Cullen asked.

Daniel stared at his two strapping, six-foot-plus sons. "Don't tell me you're afraid of her."

"Hell, yes," said Cullen.

Daniel squared his shoulders and crossed his arms over his chest. "More afraid of *her* than you are of *me?*"

Both boys snorted their disbelief.

"You're on your own with Mom," said Cullen, starting up the steep grade.

"We'll be doing something safe," Bryan said.

Cullen nodded his concurrence. "Like skydiving."

"He is making me very nervous," said Amanda to her ex-sister-in-law Karen Elliott where they sat in the solarium at The Tides, her former in-laws' palatial estate. Since her mastectomy this past winter, Karen had been recuperating out on the Long Island estate. Rays of sunlight streamed through the skylights, glowing against the hardwood floor and bringing out the pastels in the cushions covering the wicker furniture.

"Did he actually do anything?" asked Karen. A cup of herb tea in hand, she was reclining on a lounger next to the glass wall that overlooked the Atlantic. Seagulls soared on the rising air currents while storm clouds gathered on the far horizon.

"He suggested an extreme makeover." Amanda still bristled at Daniel's nerve.

"Like plastic surgery?" asked Karen.

"Like a haircut and a new wardrobe. But who knows what all else he had in mind."

"Whew." Karen blew out a breath. "You scared me for a minute. I thought maybe Sharon had completely corrupted him."

Amanda cringed at the mention of Daniel's recent ex-wife. Rail thin and strikingly beautiful, Sharon Styles was never anything less than a perfectly coiffed fashion plate.

Karen smoothed a hand over the colorful scarf that disguised the hair loss from her chemotherapy. "Personally, I'd kill for a good makeover."

Amanda gave a chopped laugh of disbelief. Karen didn't need a makeover. She was classy and gorgeous under any circumstances, from the glow of her honey-toned nose to the shine of her pedicured nails.

"I say we skip the makeover and kill off Daniel," said Amanda.

Karen suddenly sat up on the chaise, swinging her legs around the side and clinking her china teacup into its saucer. "That's exactly what I'm going to do."

Amanda feigned delight. "You're going to kill off Daniel?"

"I'm going to get a makeover. And Daniel's right. You should come with me."

"Hey!" Bad enough when Daniel criticized her appearance. She didn't need Karen jumping on the bandwagon.

Karen waved a dismissive hand. "Don't be so sensitive. We'll spend the weekend at Eduardo's. Mud wraps, facials…" Her hand went to her chest, and she rolled her eyes reverently. "Oh, one of those heated stone massages will make you feel like a new woman."

"I don't want to be a new woman. And I can't afford Eduardo's. One of those heated stone massages would bankrupt me. I don't *need* a makeover."

"When did need have anything to do with a makeover? And you can make Daniel pay."

Daniel pay? Let Daniel and his money anywhere near her life? Was Karen out of her mind?

"After all, it was his idea," said Karen with a calculating gleam.

Amanda shook her head. "I think you're missing the point of this conversation."

Karen grinned unrepentantly. "I'm not missing the point. They nuked my cancer, not my brain."

Amanda leaned forward in her armchair, folding her hands on the knees of her khaki pants, making sure she was perfectly clear this time. "I don't want to humor Daniel. I want your husband to help me get him off my back."

Karen copied Amanda's posture. "Maybe Daniel will get off your back if you get a makeover."

"If I get a makeover, Daniel will think I've taken his advice."

"Who cares?"

"*I* do. He wants me to stop practicing law. I give in on the makeover, you can bet what's coming next."

"It's not like he can have you disbarred."

Amanda paused. She supposed that was true enough. He couldn't actually force her to stop working. Could he? The Elliotts were powerful, but she had to believe there were limits on what they could pull off.

He'd have to catch her doing something unethical—which she wouldn't. Or he'd have to set her up—which he wouldn't. Her folded hands tightened. But Patrick might. If Daniel asked him to.

Of course, Patrick couldn't care less what Amanda did for a living, or whether she consorted with criminals. By the same token, neither should Daniel. Really, where on earth was this coming from?

Karen sat back in the chaise and gave an exaggerated sigh into the silence, smoothing the palm of her hand over her forehead. "I think a makeover would help me recover *so* much faster." She turned her head toward Amanda and shamelessly blinked her long lashes. "But I really don't want to go to Eduardo's all alone."

Amanda wasn't fooled for a second.

Karen was milking the situation for all it was worth. But she *had* been through a terrible illness. And if she wanted company at a weekend spa, how could Amanda refuse?

A gull cried against the sheer cliffs outside, a second answering it as the surf roiled up against the rocks.

"If I say yes," Amanda ventured, "we can't tell Daniel." If Daniel thought she was taking his advice, any of his advice, there'd be no stopping him.

A beautiful smile grew on Karen's face. "I say we let them dye your hair."

"No, we're not…" When Karen's expression faltered, Amanda paused. "You think I should dye my hair?"

"Oh, they can give you the most divine highlights. You'll love it. I promise."

Amanda didn't want divine highlights, and she sure didn't want to touch Daniel's advice with a ten-foot pole. But she did love Karen, and she supposed highlights wouldn't kill her.

"Okay. Highlights it is."

Karen all but bounced back up into a sitting position. "Great. My treat."

"No way." Amanda wasn't about to let Karen pick up the tab.

"Okay. Michael's treat. I'll make the reservations." Karen reached for the phone.

"Your husband doesn't pay, either."

"But you said—"

"Final offer. We go to Eduardo's, I pay my way and nobody tells Daniel."

"Yes! We have a plan."

Three

Daniel was a man with a plan. Of course, Daniel was always a man with a plan. But this one was better than most.

The door opened, and Cullen entered the office on the nineteenth floor of the Elliott Publication Holdings building. He tossed a sheaf of papers on Daniel's desk. "The new sales figures."

"Thanks," said Daniel, giving the report only a cursory glance.

Regina and Hopkins were probably his best bet. They were a reputable firm specializing in corporate law. He supposed getting Amanda a job offer up-front was probably too heavy-handed, but maybe he could drop a few hints regarding their billable hours and their profit margin. He was pretty sure Taylor Hopkins would give him that information.

"Last month's numbers look iffy," said Cullen, cocking his head in an effort to make eye contact. "We're not going to pull ahead with numbers like these." He paused. "It's so frustrating not knowing where we are in the competition."

"I see," said Daniel with a nod.

Amanda obviously didn't understand the amount of money to be made in corporate law. Or the fact that the money was all made during business hours. If she was invited anywhere in the evening, it would be to an art museum opening or a new production of *La Bohème*.

Daniel was willing to bet Taylor Hopkins had never, not even once, been called out at midnight to drop by the Fifty-Third Street lockup and arrange bail for a drug dealer.

"Dad?"

Not even once.

"Dad?"

Daniel blinked up at his son. "Yeah?"

"We're probably losing this race."

"You have your Mom's phone number programmed into your cell?"

Cullen didn't respond.

"Never mind," said Daniel, pressing the intercom button. "Nancy? Can you get me the number for Amanda Elliott, Attorney? She's in Midtown."

"Right away," came Nancy's voice.

"You're calling Mom?" asked Cullen.

"Somebody has to."

"Dad, I really think you need to back up and—"

"You said something about sales figures?"

"Oh, *now* you want to talk sales figures."

"When have I not wanted to talk sales figures?"

Cullen rolled his eyes. "We're not gaining any ground."

"We expected that."

Cullen pointed to a number on the top sheet. "This is a problem."

Daniel glanced down. That was a low number all right. "How are hits on the new Web site?"

"Increasing."

"People buying subscriptions?"

Cullen nodded.

"Demographics?"

"Eighteen to twenty-four is the fastest growing sector."

"Good."

"Not fast enough," said Cullen.

The intercom buzzed. "I have that number for you," said Nancy.

"I'll be right out." Daniel stood up and clapped his son on the shoulder. "Keep up the good work."

"But, Dad…"

Daniel slipped his suit jacket off the hanger on the corner coatrack.

"You're leaving?" asked Cullen, glancing from the sales report to Daniel and back again.

"I'm thinking you're right. A phone call is probably a bad idea." He'd drop by Amanda's office. That way she'd have a harder time saying no to a drink. He could call Taylor Hopkins from the car and have the facts and figures all ready to present.

Cullen walked backward, keeping himself between Daniel and the office door. "The reps will be expecting a conference call."

"We can conference call tomorrow."

Cullen came up against the door, effectively blocking Daniel's escape. "You do realize we're losing hope of catching Finola?"

"We'll make it up in Web sales. That was the strategy all along."

Cullen paused. "You do realize you're on a suicide mission with Mom?"

Daniel cracked a small smile. "Your faith in me is inspiring."

"Just laying out the facts for you."

"Your mother's an intelligent woman. She'll listen to reason."

Cullen put a hand on the doorknob. "What makes you think your idea is remotely reasonable?"

Daniel peered at his son. "Of course it's reasonable."

Cullen shook his head, his tone mocking. "Dad, Dad, Dad."

Daniel held up his index finger. "Watch yourself. I may not be able to spank you, but I can still fire you."

"You fire me, Finola will wax your ass for sure."

Daniel pushed Cullen's hand off the knob. "Young punk."

"You got your will in order?"

"I'm writing you out of it in the car."

Cullen gave him a mock salute and cocky grin as he stepped out of the way. "You're making a bold move here, Dad. A lesser man would be quaking in his boots."

Daniel hesitated for a split second.

Then he shook his head and opened the office door. He had twenty years of wisdom and experience on Cullen, and his younger son wasn't going to make him second-guess his plan.

Daniel noticed right away that Amanda's office was a startling contrast to EPH. It was smaller, darker, and where the Elliott building had lobby security, Amanda's storefront door opened directly into the reception area, inviting any passerby to come right on in.

The young, multiearringed, purple-haired receptionist didn't look as though she could stop a grandmother, never mind a criminal punk intent on harm. She stopped chewing her gum long enough to cock her head sideways in an inquiry.

"I'd like to speak with Amanda Elliott," said Daniel.

The girl indicated the closed, frosted glass office door with her thumb. "She's with Timmy the Trench. Be about five or so."

"Thank you," said Daniel.

The receptionist blew a pink bubble.

After checking a vinyl chair in the waiting room for dirt smears or chewing gum, Daniel sat down and sighed. The woman hadn't even asked his name or his business with Amanda.

When the majority of your clientele was likely armed and dangerous, a person would think rudimentary security questions would be in order. First thing Daniel would do was install a metal detector at the entrance, and maybe station a couple of former Green Berets on the sidewalk.

A meeting with Timmy the Trench.

Nobody named Timmy the Trench could be up to anything remotely legal.

Fifteen minutes later, while, out of desperation, Daniel was leafing through a six-month-old edition of a competitor's magazine, a short, balding man in a trench coat shuffled out of Amanda's office.

"Can you call Courthouse Admin?" called Amanda through the open door. "I need to know the new trial date for Timmy."

"Sure," called the receptionist, punching the numbers on her phone with long, dark fingernails.

She glanced Daniel's way and gestured to the open door. "Go on in."

Daniel rolled to his feet, tossed the magazine back on the untidy pile and headed into Amanda's office. He couldn't shake the knowledge that he could be anyone, after anything.

"Daniel?" Amanda lifted her chin, rolling back a few inches on her office chair.

"Yeah." He pushed on the door, and it rattled into place behind him. "And you're damn lucky it *is* me."

Her eyebrows shot up. "I am?"

He took one of the two molded plastic guest chairs opposite her desk. "That receptionist would have let anyone in here."

Amanda tucked her dark brown hair behind her ear. "I suppose we could issue membership cards."

He frowned. "You're being sarcastic."

"Am I? Care to guess why?"

Daniel leaned back and flicked open the button on his suit jacket. "It's a defense mechanism. You use it when I'm right and you're wrong."

"When has that ever happened?"

"I have a list of dates."

"I just bet you do."

He paused, taking in the flash of her mocha eyes. She liked this. Hell, *he* liked this. There was nobody on the planet who could spar with him like Amanda.

She was quick on her feet and downright brilliant. That much hadn't changed.

He remembered Cullen's parting words. Perhaps he had underestimated how easy it would be to lure her over to corporate law. But he was definitely giving it his best shot.

"Have dinner with me," he said on impulse. Then he saw her expression and realized his tactical error. Too bold, too up-front. It almost sounded like a date.

"Daniel—"

"With Cullen and Misty," he quickly put in. As the boss, he could order their son to join them, right? If that didn't work, he'd go straight to Misty. He'd heard through the family grapevine that she and Amanda had hit it off extremely well.

Amanda's eyes settled into a glow. "Have you seen Misty?

"No, but I saw Cullen earlier today."

"And everything's all right with the pregnancy?"

"Everything's fine." Not that Daniel had specifically asked. But Cullen would have told him if anything was wrong. Right?

Amanda picked up a pen and tapped an open spot between two file folders and her Rolodex. "So, what can I do for you, Daniel?"

"Have dinner with us."

"I mean right now."

"Now?"

"Yes, now. You went to all the trouble to come to Midtown. What do you want?"

Daniel hesitated. He hadn't planned to plunge right in, right here, right now. But what the heck, he might as well lay the groundwork. "I was talking to Taylor Hopkins earlier today."

"Let me guess, he wants my legal advice on a delicate matter."

"He's a lawyer, Amanda."

"I know he's a lawyer. I was making a joke."

Daniel shifted. "Oh, right."

She stood up.

Daniel quickly came to his feet.

She scooped up a stack of files. "Relax, Daniel. I'm just putting these away. You don't mind if I organize while you talk?"

Daniel glanced from the overflowing bookshelves to a desktop and credenza piled high with papers. "Of course not. But why doesn't Miss Gothic—"

"Julie," said Amanda.

"Fine. Julie. Why doesn't Julie do your filing?"

"She does."

Daniel scanned the room again, biting his tongue.

Amanda followed his gaze. "She's learning," she clarified.

"You mean it used to be worse?"

After some hesitation, Amanda set the pile down on a wide windowsill behind her. "Did you come here just to insult my staff?"

From his vantage point, it looked as if Amanda had blocked the air-conditioning. On a humid August day in the city. "How long has she worked here?"

"Two, two and a half—"

"Weeks?"

"Years."

"Oh."

"Don't 'oh' me like that."

"Like what?"

"Just because Elliott Publication Holdings restricts its administrative staff to Ph.D. candidates—"

Daniel jumped at the opening, narrow as it was. "I wasn't comparing you to EPH."

She arched a brow.

"I was comparing you to Regina and Hopkins."

The brow arched higher. "Who won?"

"Amanda—"

"Seriously, Daniel. How did I stack up to a cold, calculating, profit-obsessed, inhuman firm like Regina and Hopkins?"

Whoa. Where had that come from? Daniel blinked at his ex-wife.

She scooped up another armload of files and glanced around. "Thought so."

From what he could see, she was randomly rearranging the mess.

Or maybe she was nervous. Now, that wasn't a bad thing. It could give him an edge. "Why do you always treat efficiency and profit like dirty words?"

She smacked the files down on the one vacant corner of the credenza. "Because 'efficiency,' as you so carefully term it, is an excuse to treat people as profit generators."

Daniel shifted that through his brain for a second. "People *are* profit generators. You hire good people, you pay them a fair salary and they make money for your company."

"And who decides who the good people are?"

"Amanda—"

"Who decides, Daniel?"

He paused, trying to determine if it was a trick question. "The Human Resources Department," he ventured.

Amanda pointed at the office door, the edge to her tone increasing. "Julie is a good person."

"I believe you." He nodded, realizing he needed to pull back. Their arguments escalated so quickly, it was difficult to keep the conversation on an even keel.

"She might not be the best typist or filer in the world. And she'd never make it past the screeners at EPH, but she's a very good person."

"I said I believe you," Daniel repeated in a conciliatory tone, gesturing for her to sit back down.

Amanda drew a breath and plunked into her chair. "She deserves a chance."

Daniel sat, too. "Where did you find her?" He was pretty sure it wasn't through any of the reputable employment agencies.

"She's a former client."

"Is she a criminal?"

"An *accused* criminal. Jeez, Daniel. Just because they arrest you, it doesn't mean you're guilty."

"What was she accused of?"

Amanda's lips pursed for a split second. "Embezzlement."

Daniel stared at her in stunned amazement. "Embezzlement?"

"You heard me."

He stood up, taking a few steps across the small room, trying desperately to keep his composure. "You hired an *embezzler* to run your law office?"

"I said she was *accused.*"

"Was she innocent?"

"There were extenuating circumstances—"

"Amanda!"

Her eyes hardened defensively. "This is really none of your business, Daniel."

Daniel clamped his jaw. He could see how she might have that perspective. They'd gotten off on the wrong foot again. It was his fault. He should have orchestrated the conversation more carefully.

He sat down. Then he leaned forward. "You have a soft spot, Amanda. You always have."

She leaned over the desk, looking directly into his eyes. "If by a 'soft spot' you mean I look at people as more than drones, you're right."

He clamped his jaw, resisting the urge to respond.

She linked her fingers together and stretched them out as if warming up for a fight. "You want to critique my hiring practices? Let's take a quick look at yours."

"My people are the best," he said.

"Yeah? Tell me about some of your people."

"My secretary, Nancy, has a college degree in business administration, and she's an expert with computerized office tools."

Amanda lifted her pen again, tapping it rhythmically on the desk. "Does she have any kids?"

"I don't know."

"Is she married?"

Daniel thought about that. "I don't think so." Nancy never had a problem working late. If she had a husband and a family, it might bother her more.

"Here's a pop quiz for you, Daniel. Give me the name of an employee's spouse. Any employee's spouse."

"Misty."

"That's cheating."

Daniel grinned. "You did say *any* of them."

"You know what your problem is?"

"I'm smarter than you are?"

She tossed the pen at him.

He ducked.

"You have no soul," she said.

For some reason, her words hit harder than they should have. "I guess that is a problem," he said softly.

She flinched at his expression, but then quickly recovered. "I mean you are so myopically focused on business and productivity and profit, you forget the world is full of people. Your employees have their own lives. They're not just extras in yours."

"I know they have their own lives."

"In the abstract, yes. But you know nothing about those lives."

"I know everything I need to know."

"Yeah?" she asked with skepticism.

"Yeah."

"Let's contrast, shall we? Ask me something about Julie."

"Julie?"

Amanda rolled her eyes. "The Goth receptionist."

"Oh, Julie."

Amanda waited.

Daniel searched his mind for a relevant question. "Does she have any previous convictions for embezzlement?"

Amanda sat back in her chair. "No. She has an apartment in the East Village. She has an on-again, off-again boyfriend named Scott. I think she's too good for him. She's taking night school courses in spreadsheet applications. Her mother is battling arthritis, and she has two nephews, from her sister Robin, that she takes to the zoo on Saturday afternoons."

"Yet, she can't file."

"Daniel!"

"I don't see your point, Amanda. She's your employee, not your best friend."

Amanda shook her head and pulled open a desk drawer, turning her attention to the jumbled contents. "Of course you wouldn't see my point," she muttered. "You hired Sharon."

"Whoa." Daniel's shoulders tensed. His ex-wife had nothing to do with this. "That was out of line."

"How is it out of line?"

"I didn't *hire* Sharon."

Amanda glanced back up. "Be honest, Daniel. Did you marry Sharon because you loved her sense of humor, her opinions on literature and her outlook on global events?" Her voice rose. "Or did you marry her because she could make small talk in three languages, whip up canapés in under an hour and she looked great in anything by Dior?"

"I divorced Sharon."

"What happened? The canapés get soggy?"

Daniel stood. "I shouldn't have come." He hadn't meant to upset Amanda. And he sure hadn't meant to talk about Sharon. Sharon was out of his life for good.

"Why did you come, Daniel?"

"It wasn't to talk about Sharon."

Amanda nodded. "Of course not." Her eyes softened to that mocha color he loved. "I'm sorry. Do you miss her?"

"I divorced her."

"But still—"

"I don't miss Sharon. Not for one second. Not for one nanosecond." Which, when he really thought about it, meant Amanda could be right. He frowned.

She stood up and moved around the end of her desk. "So it *was* the small talk and designer gowns."

"You've got me on the ropes, and you're willing to score points?"

"Absolutely."

Daniel sighed. What had attracted him to Sharon in the first place? His father had supported the marriage, but that couldn't have been all there was to it.

He was recovering from losing Amanda at the time. Maybe he simply hadn't cared whom he married. Maybe he thought

Sharon would be a safer wife. A wife that knew his world and wouldn't expect things from him that he simply couldn't deliver.

Like Amanda had.

"Daniel?" Amanda's voice interrupted his thoughts.

He focused on her face. She'd moved closer, and he could smell her perfume. "Yeah?"

"I asked you when."

"When what?"

Her mouth curved into a patient smile. "Dinner with Cullen and Misty?"

He stared at her smile. She was still so incredibly beautiful, with full lips, shiny hair, bottomless eyes.

He shifted from one foot to the other. "Oh. Friday, eight o'clock at The Premier."

"Sure."

"Good." He had a sudden urge to touch her hair. He'd always loved running his fingers through its scented, silky softness. It was one of his favorite things in the world.

"Daniel?"

He curled his fingers into fists to keep them still. "Yeah?"

"I'm sorry I brought up Sharon."

"Do you really think I hired her to be my wife?" He was genuinely curious.

"I think your priorities are mixed-up."

"How?"

She paused. "You're a very driven man, Daniel."

"Yeah? Well you're what's driving me crazy at the moment."

She tilted her head and a slow grin formed on her lips. "Then you should stop hunting me down."

"You're probably right about that," he breathed, daring to move a little closer. "But, apparently, I find you irresistible."

Her eyes widened.

He touched her hair—stopped fighting the compulsion and simply reached out. His fingers released its scent, and he was catapulted back fifteen years. "I'm trying to help you here, Amanda."

Her voice was breathless. "I don't need any help."

"Yes, you do." He kissed her lightly on the forehead. "And lucky for you, I'm available."

As the office door rattled shut behind Daniel, Amanda grabbed the corner of her desk for support.

I'm available?

What did that mean? *I'm available.*

And why had he kissed her?

Okay, so he hadn't exactly kissed her. But he had—

"Amanda?" The office door opened, and Julie stuck her head in the room. Her brows waggled and a secretive smile curved her dark purple lips.

"So, who was hubba hubba man?"

Amanda stared at her blankly.

"The guy who just left," Julie elaborated.

"Daniel?"

"Right." Julie mimicked a swoon. "Delectable Daniel."

"He's my ex-husband."

Julie drew back. "Hello? You *exed* that guy?"

"I did."

"What were you thinking?"

"That he was uptight, pretentious and controlling."

"Who cares?"

Good question. No, bad question. Amanda had left Daniel for some very good reasons, not the least of which were his single-minded desire for success and his refusal to maintain even the slightest independence from his father.

"I cared," she said to Julie.

Julie shook her head and gave an exaggerated sigh. "To each his own, I guess. So what did he want?"

Amanda pressed her fingertips into her temple. "To run my life."

"Going to let him?"

"Not a chance."

"Going to see him again?"

"Nope." Well, not after Friday. And that didn't count, since Cullen and Misty would be there.

Julie shrugged. "Okay, then. Your two o'clock's here."

Amanda glanced at her watch. "It's nearly two-thirty."

"I didn't want to disturb you."

She gave Julie a gentle shove toward the doorway. "He's a paying client. Disturb me already."

Julie strained to look back over her shoulder. "I thought you might be jumping Mr. Delectable on the desktop."

"Yeah, right," said Amanda, ignoring the rise in her pulse.

Julie chuckled low. "That's what I would have done."

Four

Amanda slid the hanger of her red Chaiken silk along the rod at the far end of her closet. She didn't mind that it was several years out of date. She *did* mind that it was too sultry for an evening in the same room as Daniel.

Next she peered at the V-necked Vera Wang. Nope. Too Vegas.

Then she frowned at the sequined Tom Ford. Nope again. Too princess.

Her ten-year-old, multicolored Valentino sunburst was the last one on the rack. As far as comfort went, it left a lot to be desired. It was strapless, and she'd have to wear one of those underwire torture devices to keep her breasts in the right position. But it was made of beautiful orange, yellow and red-streaked silk, snug across the bodice, with a flowing skirt and a scalloped hem that was very flattering.

It was elegant, without giving in to basic, New York black.

She glanced at her watch. Oops. For better or worse, this was the dress.

Tossing it on the bed, she headed for the shower. A light was blinking on the answering machine, but she ignored it. She'd stayed too late at the office reading a brief, and now she had five minutes to wash her hair, throw on a little makeup and strap herself into the torture underwear.

Halfway through the shampoo, she remembered she also needed shoes. More specifically, she needed those little gold sandals with the crossover straps.

They were in the front hall closet…maybe.

So much for makeup.

She ducked her head under the spray, scrubbing her nails furiously against her scalp. Then she shut off the tap, rubbed her skin with a towel and headed for the entry hall.

She dropped to her knees on the soft carpet in front of her closet and scrambled through the untidy pile of shoes. Black, beige, flats, sneakers…

Ah ha. Little gold sandals. Well, one, anyway.

She hunted for the other, coming up lucky.

She threw them by the door and dashed back to her room.

She snapped on the bra and stepped into a matching pair of panties. Thank goodness she'd shaved her legs this morning. Lately, she hadn't been as diligent about that as she should.

She shimmied into the dress, pathetically grateful when the zipper slipped up easily. In the bathroom she ran a comb through her hair. In the hallway, she stuffed her feet into sandals. Finally, she was set.

Purse.

Darn. She ran back to the bedroom and grabbed an evening purse. She spied a pair of garnet earrings on the dresser and slid them through her pierced ears.

There.

That had to be it.

Her hair would dry in the taxi.

She grabbed her keys and headed out the front door.

"Ms. Elliott?" A uniformed chauffeur was waiting at the bottom of the stairs beside a stretch limousine.

Amanda's steps faltered. "Yes?"

He opened the back door with a flourish. "With Mr. Elliott's compliments, ma'am."

Amanda stared at the car.

"He apologizes if you didn't get the phone message."

Amanda's first instinct was to send the limo back to Daniel. But then she mentally shrugged. Why chase down a taxi out of spite?

She smiled at the driver and crossed the sidewalk. "Thank you."

"Of course," said the driver with a nod.

Amanda peeked inside at a bar, a television, three phones and a video-game controller. It had definitely been a while since she'd ridden in this kind of luxury.

She glanced back at the driver. "I don't suppose you have a hair dryer in there."

The driver grinned. "Afraid not. Do you need a few more minutes?"

"No thank you. I'm already late."

"A lady's prerogative," he said.

She shook her head and stepped into the car. "They'll just have to take me as I am."

"You look lovely, ma'am," he said diplomatically.

"Thank you," Amanda returned, making herself comfortable on the bench seat. "And thank you for picking me up."

"My pleasure." He closed the door.

The limo glided smoothly away from the curb. Low purple lights came on around the perimeter and soft music floated out from unseen speakers.

"Would you care for a beverage?" asked the driver.

"No, thank you." Amanda leaned back and watched the surrealistic blur of traffic lights through the tinted windows. She really shouldn't enjoy this quite so much.

"Mr. Elliott asked me to apologize about the mix-up with the restaurant," the driver continued.

"Mix-up?" asked Amanda, straightening.

"He wasn't able to get reservations at The Premier."

Amanda hid a small grin. An Elliott turned down by a maître d'? That must have driven Daniel wild.

"So, where are we going?" she asked.

"To Mr. Elliott's apartment."

"His apartment?"

The driver nodded in the mirror. "Yes, ma'am."

Amanda's hand splayed on her stomach. Whew. Okay. Deep breath. She could do this.

Misty and Cullen would be there as a buffer. And there'd probably be a dozen or so kitchen staff. It wasn't as if she and Daniel would get all cozy on the balcony or anything.

It wasn't a date.

Although he *had* kissed her.

On the forehead.

Still, his lips had touched her skin.

She dropped her head into her hands.

"Ma'am…"

She straightened, flipping her damp hair back from her face. "I'm fine. It's nothing."

"Are you sure?"

"I'm sure." She gave him a reassuring smile.

She'd go to Daniel's apartment. Have dinner. Chat with her son and new daughter-in-law, maybe feel the baby kick then get out of there before things got awkward.

Simple.

* * *

Things got awkward faster than she'd expected.

"Misty wasn't feeling well," said Daniel as he closed the front door in an oak-paneled, skylighted entry hall.

"So they're not coming at all?" Amanda darted a glance at the exit, wondering if she should bolt before it was too late.

"Her back was sore."

Misty's health was definitely more important than dinner, but Amanda had been counting on their presence. An evening alone with Daniel was more than she could handle right now. "Why didn't you call?"

"I did call. I left you a message."

"Then why did you send the car?"

"The message was that we'd moved to my place, not that you weren't supposed to come."

"But…"

He gestured to the short staircase leading to his sunken living room. "Please come in."

She hesitated. But there was no way to bail without looking scared. And she wasn't scared. Not exactly.

"Amanda?"

She took a bracing breath, made her decision then stepped down the short staircase to the plush ivory carpet.

The room was nothing short of magnificent. Two stories high, it was decorated with sculptures and abstract oils. Camel-colored sofas were scattered with burgundy and navy cushions, alongside two plaid armchairs that formed a conversation group.

Pot lights were sunk into the high ceiling. There was a Monet above a white marble fireplace, flanked by two walls of double-decker windows overlooking the park.

The furniture gleamed, and the flower arrangements were fresh. A team of photographers could show up for a lifestyle shoot and not have to touch a thing.

52   MARRIAGE TERMS

"I ran into Taylor Hopkins earlier," said Daniel, crossing the huge room to a curved cherrywood bar.

"Oh?" Amanda took a cautious step forward. Even for Daniel, the room was pristine. There wasn't a single magazine on the tables, no papers, no dust, not even a track in the carpet. She wondered if it was Sharon's influence, or if he was spiraling down to some sort of perfection psychosis.

He retrieved two wineglasses from the hanging rack. "He was free, so I invited him to dinner."

Amanda's gaze shot to Daniel's back. "You invited who to dinner? When?"

"Taylor."

"Why?"

"Because he was free."

Taylor was free? The same Taylor that Daniel had mentioned on Tuesday? The same Taylor he'd held up as an example of lawyerly perfection?

"What are you up to?" she asked warily.

"Opening the wine. You want some?"

"You're telling me you accidentally ran into Taylor *after* Misty called?" She didn't believe anything in Daniel's life was random.

His shoulders tensed. "After *Cullen* called," he corrected. Then he relaxed and turned his head to look at her. "Glass of merlot?"

"Daniel, what's going on?"

He shrugged as he twisted the corkscrew into the wine. "Nothing's going on."

Yeah, right. "Why is Taylor really coming to dinner?"

"Because Stuart had already picked up the salmon, and because you and I were going to be alone." He popped the cork.

Alone? If alone was a problem for him, why hadn't he canceled?

A man in a white suit jacket entered the room. "May I help with the drinks, sir?"

"Thanks," said Daniel, abandoning the open bottle to the perfectly groomed gentleman.

"We could have rebooked," said Amanda.

"Then who would eat the salmon?"

Her eyes narrowed. There was something suspicious about that straightforward logic, but she couldn't quite put her finger on it.

"Care for a tour before dinner?" he asked easily, not a flicker of cunning in his eyes.

Maybe she was being paranoid. Maybe Daniel wasn't thinking up plans to interfere in her life. Maybe she'd over-estimated his interest entirely.

"Okay," she agreed slowly.

The man in the white jacket handed them each a glass of merlot.

"Thank you, Stuart," said Daniel.

"Thank you," Amanda echoed.

"Dinner in an hour?" asked Stuart.

"Sounds fine," said Daniel.

Then he placed his hand lightly at the small of her back. "Let's start upstairs."

Amanda forced herself to relax and take in the decor. The room smelled of beeswax and lemon polish. She ran her fingertips gingerly along the gleaming banister as they climbed the stairs.

When they stepped onto the landing, Daniel directed her along the hallway that overlooked the living room.

"Your house is very…neat," she offered.

There was a hint of a chuckle in his voice. "Why do I get the feeling that wasn't a compliment?"

"I don't know," she lied.

"You'd prefer it was messy?" he asked.

She'd prefer it had a soul. "Well, my house is definitely a lot messier than yours."

"Do you have a housekeeper?"

She glanced up at him. "Why?"

He didn't meet her eyes. "Just wondering if you might have hired a former client to do that, too."

Amanda resisted the urge to elbow him in the ribs. "I don't have a housekeeper."

"I see."

No rebuke. Nothing overt that she could fight with. Just a measured, judgmental *I see.*

"Regular people clean their own houses," she pointed out.

He opened a door and hit the light switch. "This is the library."

She gazed at another pristine room. Two leather love seats faced each other across an antique table. There was a reading desk in the corner with a diamond-tufted chair. And a lighted, saltwater fish tank was built into floor-to-ceiling bookshelves. The wood was deep and rich, in contrast to the muted neutrals in the living room and hall.

She wandered inside, running her finger along the leather-bound volumes.

"Shakespeare," said Daniel.

Of course it was. "Got anything lighter?"

"A first edition Dickens."

"Anything newer?"

"The Life of Pi."

"I give up." Maybe it wasn't an act. Maybe Daniel had truly turned into a paragon of perfection. His father must be proud.

"You give what up?" he asked.

"Mr. Elliott?" Stuart appeared in the doorway. "Your company has arrived."

"Thank you." Daniel smiled at Amanda and gestured to the library doorway.

"Taylor," he greeted over the railing. "Glad you could make it."

"Wouldn't miss it," Taylor responded, smiling at Amanda as she and Daniel made their way down the stairs.

"Amanda," he said, holding out his hand.

She reached out to shake.

"You probably don't remember," he said, grasping her hand warmly. "We met at a party once. Karen and Michael introduced us."

"The Ritz," said Amanda. She remembered. He'd been polite and friendly that night, with a quick smile and a courteous manner that made it hard to remember he was a cold, unfeeling profitmonger.

"You *do* remember." He flashed that boyish grin and prolonged the handshake.

"Merlot?" asked Daniel.

Taylor slowly let go of Amanda's hand, keeping his gaze fixed on her eyes. "Love some."

Daniel couldn't let Taylor's interest in Amanda bother him. Sure, he'd only invited the man over to talk business, not to gaze adoringly into Amanda's eyes and chuckle appreciatively every time she said something that remotely resembled a joke.

And he hadn't expected Taylor to pat her hand, touch her arm or inquire about her personal life. But Amanda was an attractive, sexy woman, particularly when her hair got disheveled and she kicked off her sandals to curl her legs up on the couch.

Daniel had to accept the fact that other men were going to find her interesting. He couldn't let it bother him.

Even now, when Taylor stood up and oh so casually offered Amanda a ride home, Daniel had to bite his tongue and set his jaw. None of his business if she wanted to accept.

Amanda glanced at him.

He kept his expression deliberately impassive.

"Thank you, no," she said to Taylor.

And Taylor accepted her answer with equanimity.

Daniel saw Taylor to the front door alone, trying to keep the spring out of his step. Her relationships with other men were irrelevant. He had to focus on the primary goal— getting her to change careers.

He thanked Taylor sincerely for joining them.

When he returned to the living room, Amanda was still curled up on the couch, sipping a second cup of coffee.

"I hope you had a nice time," he said, retaking his seat in the armchair across from her.

"Nice coincidence, you running into him at Boca Royce." Daniel nodded. "It was."

"And so interesting, all those little details about his business," she continued.

He met her eyes. "I know I found them interesting."

"I had no idea corporate law was so easy and so lucrative."

"Makes me wish I'd become a lawyer," he joked.

"Me, too. Wait. I *did* become a lawyer."

Daniel grinned. She was fun when she relaxed.

"And, you know…" Amanda snapped her fingers. "Listening to Taylor makes me wonder why I've spent my entire career on criminal defense."

Daniel tried not to act too interested. "It does?"

She nodded vigorously. "Think about it, if I'd gone into corporate law right off, I could have a new Mercedes by now."

"You could," he agreed, with what he hoped was a thoughtful nod. He'd have to thank Taylor again tomorrow. The man had obviously hit exactly the right note.

"And I could sleep in every morning, get the best theatre tickets from clients and shop for clothes on Fifth Avenue."

Daniel rested his hands on the arms of his chair, trying not to look too eager. "*Snap* would be happy to give you some business, and an excellent recommendation."

Amanda bobbed her head up and down. "That would help. And I bet you could get me some uptown office space, too."

"Sure," said Daniel. He was surprised, delighted, actually, by the turn of the conversation.

"And you could rent a van, maybe pack up my files."

"I'd be happy to help in—"

"Heck, you could probably hire somebody to blow off my existing clients."

Uh-oh. Her dark eyes began to glitter, and Daniel's stomach slid down a few inches. "I…"

"And find me a new receptionist."

Daniel felt like a supreme fool. "You're yanking my chain, aren't you?"

She came to her feet. "Of course I'm yanking your chain! Did you really think that setup would work?"

Yeah, actually. Daniel rose. "I'd—"

"That Taylor Hopkins is a one-man press gang."

Okay, salvage time. What could he say? What could he do? "I was only thinking—"

"Yeah, yeah." She waved a hand. "You were only thinking about me. Tell me, Daniel, were Cullen and Misty ever really invited?"

He flinched. He hadn't expected that to come up again. He'd thought about inviting them, but it just seemed simpler to go straight to Taylor.

Amanda's hands went to her hips. "I knew it. Will you lay off my life? I'm doing perfectly fine, thank you very much."

"But—"

"No *buts.*" She jabbed a finger at him. "You back off."

"Okay." At least temporarily.

She dropped her hand, a look of surprise coming over her face. "You will?"

He shrugged. "Sure." It wasn't as if arguing with her tonight was going to get him anywhere.

She gave a sharp nod. "Good choice." Then her voice dropped to a mumble. "It's not like *your* life is working out so well."

Daniel squared his shoulders. "Excuse me?"

"Nothing."

"That wasn't nothing."

"Fine. I said it's not like your life is working out so well."

"You're going to have to explain that one."

"Look around you," she gestured with her hand.

He looked around, and what he saw was—not to put too fine a point on it—pretty darned decent. "What exactly about this isn't working out so well?"

"It's pristine. It's perfect. There's absolutely no life in your life."

He squinted. "You win many court cases with arguments like that?"

She cocked her head and crossed her arms over her chest, pushing up her breasts.

Cleavage. Okay, that was helpful. He'd really be able to concentrate now.

"I'm beginning to think you need professional help," she said.

For a moment he was speechless. *She* was worried about *him?*

"You're the one whose life is out of control," he pointed out.

"At least I know what I want," she countered.

Ha. He had her now. If there was one thing Daniel's life had, it was direction. "I know exactly what I want."

"What's that?"

He took the easiest answer. "To be CEO of Elliott Publication Holdings."

"Do you, Daniel?"

"Of course." Just because success wasn't on Amanda's to-do list, didn't mean it wasn't on his. "Can we go back to talking about you now?"

"No. I'm not the one with the problem."

Daniel scoffed. "I've seen your office."

She scoffed right back. "And I've seen your apartment."

He opened his mouth, but then he paused, an idea twigging in his mind. She seemed fixated on his apartment. Maybe there was room to maneuver here. A deal of some kind. A swap. His apartment for her office.

"Tell me what you'd change," he said.

Her dark eyes narrowed.

He moved closer, lowering his voice. "Really. Tell me. I'm ready to take your advice."

"No, you're not."

"Yeah, I am." He moved closer still. If he took her advice, she might feel honor bound to take his. "Give it to me straight, Amanda. I can take it."

She was silent for a moment, but then her gaze turned pitying. "Okay. You want it straight? You've stopped feeling."

"Feeling what?"

"Everything."

That just plain wasn't true. Especially not now. Especially not at this particular moment.

She placed her small hand on his shoulder, and his muscle contracted beneath its warmth. "Feel," she urged.

"I am," he rasped.

Then her eyes turned mocha, and she came up on her toes. She tilted her head, parted those deep ruby lips and took his mouth against hers.

Memories saturated his brain, longing, passion, desire. He was catapulted back decades. His arms went around her, dragging her against him. He slanted his head, kissed her back, inhaling her familiar scent.

He reveled in the tender moisture of her mouth. Her body was imprinted on his brain, and his hands slid down the curve of her back, remembering. Oh, how he'd missed this. How he'd missed her.

He felt every molecule in his body hum to life. Colors and emotions swirled around in a kaleidoscope.

He let his mouth roam, and she twined her arms around his neck, her breaths puffing against his skin, nearly driving him out of his mind. He longed to lose himself in her, to tear off her clothes and lay her back right there and then on the soft carpet and relive every ounce of love they'd ever found in each other.

Her small moan vibrated against his mouth.

He whispered that he wanted her, so much, too much.

She drew back at that, blinking her big brown eyes in obvious confusion. Her cheeks were flushed. Her lips were swollen. And her chestnut hair was a messy halo of filtered light.

There'd never been a more desirable woman. Ever.

But she wasn't his.

She hadn't been his for a very long time.

He forced himself to release her.

"I'm sorry," he said. "I had no right…"

He didn't know what else to say. He never got carried away. He was the master of self-control.

An ironic half smile grew on her face. "Don't be sorry. We're making progress. You felt something."

He dropped his arms and stepped completely away. "That was *therapy?*"

She shrugged. "Of course."

Something inside him froze. That was what the kiss was to her? A point in her argument? He'd been out there on memory lane all by himself?

Yeah, he wanted her to change careers. But there was a limit to how far he'd go. And he had a feeling he'd just reached it.

Five

Amanda tipped her head back against the smooth headrest as the limo eased into traffic. Kissing Daniel *had* been therapy.

Memory enhancement.

For her.

It was only the years of practice, keeping her control in front of sharp-eyed judges, that kept her from swooning, or begging, or worse.

Daniel had always been a great kisser. From that very first night, he'd made the earth shift beneath her and pyrotechnics shoot off inside her brain.

As the limo accelerated away from a red light, she sighed her way into the memory. Their very first kiss—prom night.

Amanda had been more of a nerd than a jock back then, more likely to be found at photography club or the social activism office on a Saturday night than at an A-list party. So when her friend Bethany had wrangled an invitation to

Roger Dawson's after-prom party in the Presidential Suite of the Riverside, there was no way in the world she was missing it.

The event was a crush. The music was loud, the punch was spiked with something bitter and the snacks were being used as missiles. Amanda had been quickly separated from Bethany, so when she spotted Daniel standing alone near the door, she was thrilled to see a semifamiliar face. She'd eased toward him, squeezing her way between dancing couples and chattering groups of friends.

She and Daniel had met on several occasions early in the year when she was dating one of his friends. He'd always struck her as a nice guy, and he knew everybody. If she was lucky, maybe he'd introduce her to a few people, and she could stop standing around looking like a dork.

"Hey, Daniel," she breathed, yanking her arm from where it was trapped between two bodies.

"Amanda." He turned and smiled warmly down at her. "I didn't know you were coming."

"I came with Bethany." She gestured vaguely in the direction Bethany had disappeared twenty minutes ago.

"Hey, Elliott?" someone called from the crowd.

"Yeah?" Daniel called back.

"You got a room, right?"

Daniel nodded over the heads of the crowd. But Amanda was too short to see whom he was talking to.

"We need your ice bucket and some more glasses," the guy called.

"I'll get 'em," said Daniel.

Amanda's heart sank. Just when she'd found someone to talk to, he was leaving.

Daniel looked back down at her. "You wanna come help?

"Yes," Amanda quickly said.

"Let's go."

Daniel elbowed them a path to the door, and they emerged into the cool, quiet hallway.

"I'm down at the end," he said.

"You didn't want to drive home?" she asked, just to make conversation.

He chuckled a little self-consciously. "My older brother Michael rented the room. He figured I might get lucky."

Amanda swallowed and tried to make her voice nonchalant. "Oh. Uh, you're, uh, here with Shelby Peterson?"

Daniel shrugged. "I thought I was. But last time I saw her, she was dancing with Roger. Maybe Roger'll be the one to get lucky."

Amanda wasn't used to talking about sex, particularly not with guys, and definitely not with great-looking jocks who'd probably slept with half the cheerleading squad. Her face grew warm.

When she didn't answer, Daniel looked down. "Hey, I'm sorry." He gave her a friendly nudge with his shoulder. "That was tacky."

She shook her head, embarrassed that she wasn't as sophisticated as his friends. "No, it wasn't."

"Yeah, it was. Here we are." He stopped and unlocked the door, swinging it wide open.

Amanda had never been in a five-star hotel before. She hadn't seen much of the Presidential Suite, because of the crowd. Now she glanced around in wide-eyed amazement at the plump, burgundy couches, a curved wooden bar with a mirrored background, double French doors leading to a bedroom and a fern-filled bay window alcove with a Jacuzzi tub.

The door swung shut behind them.

"Go ahead and look around," said Daniel, dropping his key on the entry table. "This is going to take me a couple of minutes."

"Wow," said Amanda, not even pretending to be blasé

about the opulent room. "Michael must have thought you were going to get *very* lucky."

Daniel chuckled from behind the bar. "Michael's the optimist of the family."

Amanda wandered between the two couches, glancing down at the oak coffee table. There was a fresh flower arrangement in the middle, a dish of gourmet chocolates on one end and an arrangement of current magazines on the other.

More interesting was the rectangular gadget covered in colorful buttons. "Is that a remote control?" she asked, picking it up and aiming it at the television. She'd heard about them, but had never seen one in real life.

Daniel popped his head up from where he was rattling glasses. "I don't know. Try it and see."

She pushed the power button, and the television clicked to life. "All right!"

Daniel laughed at her exclamation.

She checked out the other buttons and began clicking through channels. "I think these are going to be really popular."

"I can't find the ice bucket," said Daniel, glancing at the glass shelves behind him.

"Want me to check the bathroom?"

He rounded the end of the bar. "I'll do it. Eat some of those chocolates, will you? Michael probably paid a fortune for them."

Amanda grinned, happy to oblige. She plopped down on the soft couch and peeled the gold foil from a chocolate truffle.

It was so much nicer here—cooler air, a place to sit down, nobody shouting obscenities or throwing food, no repetitive bass pounding against her eardrums. And, best of all, no crushing mortification because she was the only person in the room without a conversation partner.

"No ice bucket," said Daniel. He stopped behind the couch. "Is that *American Graffiti?*"

Amanda glanced at the screen. "I think so."

"Cool. Are the chocolates any good?"

She rocked forward and took another gold globe from the dish. "To die for." She handed it back to Daniel.

On the screen, a group of high school grads were out celebrating their final night together.

Daniel unwrapped the chocolate and gestured to the television. "Kind of like us," he said.

Amanda nodded her agreement. Like the characters in the movie, they were standing on the cusp of a brave new world. Sometimes she was excited, mostly she was scared. Her parents had saved the money for her first year of college, but after that it was going to be a struggle.

"These are great," said Daniel, coming around the couch. He picked up the dish, plunked it down on the middle cushion and sat down on the other end. "I say we eat them before we leave."

Amanda nodded her agreement and helped herself to another chocolate. "Seems a shame to let them go to waste."

She let the sweet, creamy candy melt on her tongue as they watched the movie in silence for a few minutes.

"So, what are you going to do?" Daniel asked, snagging another chocolate.

"After the party?"

"No. After high school. You had pretty good grades, didn't you?"

Amanda nodded. Given her slow dating life, she'd had plenty of time to study. "I've been accepted to NYU."

"That's great. What are you taking?"

"English lit and prelaw. What about you?"

"The family firm," he said with a tired smile.

"Guaranteed job," she offered.

He was quiet for a couple more minutes, his eyes fixed on the movie. "You know, what I'm really hoping…"

She waited, but he didn't continue.

"What?" she finally asked.

He shook his head.

"Tell me."

He shifted one leg onto the couch and angled himself toward her. "Promise you won't laugh."

Amanda Kedrick laugh at Daniel Elliott? Not in this lifetime. She shook her head. "I'm not gonna laugh."

"Okay." He nodded. "Here's the thing. I'm hoping I can talk my dad into starting a new magazine."

Amanda was impressed. It sounded so much more interesting than plain old law school. "Really? What kind?"

"Outdoor adventures, foreign lands, action. I could travel all over the world, write articles and send them back to New York."

Amanda swallowed, suddenly feeling boring and trite. She wasn't even planning to leave the state, and here Daniel was going on a global adventure.

"You think it's a dumb idea," he said, his expression falling.

"No," Amanda quickly assured him, moving a little closer. "I think it's a fantastic idea. I'm jealous is all."

He perked up. "You are?"

She nodded vigorously. "It sounds fantastic."

He took another chocolate, grinning as he unwrapped it and popped it into his mouth. "It does, doesn't it?"

They both turned their attention to the movie again.

After a few moments he rolled to his feet and went back behind the bar. "These chocolates are making me thirsty. Ever drink champagne?"

Her eyes went wide. "Where would we get champagne?"

He held up a green bottle.

"But won't you get in trouble?"

Daniel shrugged as he twisted off the wire cork holder. "Room's in Michael's name."

"So, they'll think—"

"I don't particularly care what they think." He popped the cork with his thumbs. It hit the ceiling and bounced to the carpet.

Amanda suddenly felt very daring. "I'd love some champagne."

He grinned and flipped over two of the long-stemmed glasses on the bar. Then he poured the bubbly liquid, scooped a bag of pretzels from the snack basket and rejoined her on the couch where Ron Howard's character was fighting with his steady girlfriend.

To a backdrop of fifties music, Daniel and Amanda leaned forward and touched their glasses together.

"Happy prom night," he whispered.

She gazed into his deep blue eyes, not feeling nearly as awkward as she had earlier. "You do realize you're not going to get lucky."

His eyes sparkled and a grin curved up the corners of his mouth. "I think that ship's already sailed." He glanced down at the empty bowl between them. "I mean, since you scarfed down all the chocolates that I was going to use to seduce the girl."

She smacked him on the shoulder. "I had a little help, you know."

He gave her a mock frown. "They were my secret weapon."

Instead of answering, she took a sip of the champagne. "Hey, this is good." She held the glass up to the light and watched the tiny bubbles rise to the surface. "I think the champagne should be your secret weapon."

"Yeah? Well, you're scarfing that down, too," he complained.

She smiled around another swallow. "Life sucks sometimes, doesn't it?"

He laughed and took a drink, glancing at the television screen. "What did I miss?"

"Terry the Toad is hoping to get lucky."

"Did Richard Dreyfuss find the blonde?"

"Not yet."

Daniel tore open the bag of pretzels and settled back into the couch.

Amanda sighed with contentment. She'd hated the party. Hated to admit it, but she hated her first teenage A-list party.

This was so much better, lounging on comfortable furniture, watching a funny movie, laughing and talking with Daniel and sipping on a beverage that didn't taste like orange-flavored gasoline.

She reached for a pretzel.

So much better to eat food she was positive nobody'd used as a missile.

By the time Richard Dreyfuss's character flew off in an airplane, Amanda had kicked off her shoes and the champagne bottle was half-empty.

"He never even got to meet her," Daniel complained.

They'd both editorialized throughout the movie, sharing surprise, suspense and laughter.

Amanda raised her glass. "She will forever remain the mystery woman."

"That sucks."

"It's fiction."

"It still sucks."

She laughed.

Daniel set down his glass. "A guy shouldn't let opportunities like that go by."

"Kiss ye blond bombshells while ye may?"

"Something like that."

She gathered the remains of their impromptu picnic and padded barefoot over to the bar, the carpet soft against her feet. "We should probably get back to the party," she offered reluctantly.

He stood up behind her, the glasses clinking together as he lifted them from the table. "I guess we should. We never did find the ice bucket."

"I have a feeling nobody's going to notice missing ice at this point." She turned around and came face-to-face with him, or rather face-to-chest, since he was a good six inches taller now that she wasn't wearing shoes.

He reached around her and set the glasses on the bar. "Not if they kept drinking that punch, they won't."

She shuddered again at the memory.

"Amanda?" His voice sounded unnaturally low.

She tipped up her chin to look at him. "Yes?"

He cocked his head sideways, and she was suddenly aware of a shift in the atmosphere.

"I was thinking," he said, moving almost imperceptibly closer.

His closeness should have made her feel crowded, but it didn't. His shoulders were broad. His chest was deep. And he towered over her, but she didn't feel the least bit intimidated.

She drew in a breath and smelled his spicy, masculine scent. "Thinking about what?"

"Missed opportunities." He smoothed a wisp of hair that had escaped near her temple.

She was pretty sure she wasn't misunderstanding his signals. But the thought of Daniel Elliott coming on to her was so far out in left field.

"You mean, the movie?" she asked.

"I mean graduation."

Confused, she squinted at him.

"We might never see each other again," he said.

"We might not," she agreed. Their paths barely crossed in the same school, never mind when she was at NYU and he was globe-trotting in search of exciting magazine stories.

"So…" he breathed.

"So?" she returned.

"What do we do about that?"

She watched his eyes darken, his smile fade, his lips part.

"Daniel?"

"It's now or never, Amanda." He smoothed his palm over her cheek, ever so slowly, giving her time to adjust to the change of mood, plenty of time to protest.

He twined his fingers into her hair, stroking her scalp. "I'm about to kiss you," he rasped.

"I know," she whispered, longing for his kiss.

It was perfect. It was right. Somehow she knew, intellectually, emotionally, cosmically, that this kiss at this moment was absolutely meant to be.

His lips touched hers. Firm, then tender, then moist, then hot.

She wound her arms around his neck, answering his pressure, parting her lips and tilting her head to deepen the kiss. Desire surged up inside her. She went hot, then cold, then hot all over again.

It was Daniel—Daniel Elliott—kissing her, holding her. His scent mingled with flowers. His taste overpowered the chocolate and champagne. Her skin prickled and her blood sang. She'd never felt remotely like this before.

Sparks of desire shot through her. She'd kissed boys before, but never like this, never where their touch took control of her body and soul.

She wanted it harder. She wanted it deeper. She parted her lips, inviting him in.

His tongue invaded her mouth, and she nearly whimpered with the pleasure.

His free arm circled her waist, settling across the small of her back, anchoring her firmly against his hardening body.

Yes. Closer, tighter. She wound her arms around his neck, pressing against him, tilting her head to deepen the kiss.

An ocean roared in her ears, and her hands clenched convulsively against him. The kiss went on and on. He swirled his tongue through her tender mouth. She opened wider, answering him back.

A sound emerged from deep in his chest as he arched her backward, over the bar. One strong hand traveled up her spine, traversing to settle on her rib cage, thumb barely brushing the underside of her breast. She felt her nipples tighten, sparks of pleasure shooting through her.

She wished he'd touch her, but she was too afraid to ask. Then his other hand stroked down her neck. She tensed. She waited. And then his fingertips moved to her breast. She all but bucked under the intense sensation.

"Amanda," he rasped.

Her breath came in pants and she slid her palms up his chest, slipping beneath his suit jacket, working her way to the heat of his back and pressing her breasts harder into his hands. Her world contracted to him and her.

No wonder her friends got so carried away. No wonder they made love with their boyfriends in the back seats of cars and beneath the stadium bleachers. At the moment, she couldn't have cared less where they were.

A pounding need echoed in her brain and blotted out time, space and reason.

"Daniel." Her voice turned his name into a plea.

"This is—" He kissed her again and his hands burned through her silk halter dress. His thumb circled her hardened nipple, shooting sparks to the core of her being. She never knew such sensations existed.

Gone was modesty. Gone was shyness. She wanted Daniel with every single fiber of her being. Wanted him in a way she'd never wanted anybody ever before.

He moved to her neck, kissing her roughly, fiercely, abrading her tender skin with delicious furor.

She tipped her head back to give him better access. Her breath hissed through her teeth, and she tightened her grip on his back. His jacket had to go. She wanted to touch his skin, to feel his fire.

He kissed her shoulder. His lips moved to the hollow between her breasts, and she moaned in wanting. His hands went to the halter tie at the back of her neck.

"Tell me to stop," he demanded, even as he worked the knot. He breathed her in, his hot tongue flicking out to taste her skin.

"Don't stop," she said, breathless with need. "Don't stop." Electricity pulsed at the apex of her thighs, making her nearly desperate to assuage the burning need.

"Amanda," he groaned. The bow came free, and the slinky fabric slipped down to her waist.

Daniel drew back, his gaze fixed on her bare breasts.

She arched her spine, closing her eyes, boldly raking her fingers back through her hair and shaking it loose.

Daniel swore through clenched teeth. "You're beautiful," he groaned. "Unbelievably beautiful." His hand closed over her breast, and she moaned at the intense sensation.

She felt beautiful. For the first time in her life she felt beautiful and desirable and totally unselfconscious about her body.

She pushed his jacket from his shoulders, desperate to feel his skin next to hers. She might not know much, but she did know his clothes had to go.

The jacket hit the floor, and she went to work on his tie.

He sucked in a tight breath as she loosened it.

"Amanda." His voice sounded desperate.

She kissed his mouth again, flipping open the buttons on his shirt.

"We can stop," he hissed. "It'll kill me, but we can still…"

Finally, skin. Her lips touched his bare chest, and his entire body convulsed.

"We're not stopping," she breathed against his warm skin. Of all the options in all the world, stopping right now was not one of them.

"Thank God." He found the tip of her breast and did something that made her knees nearly give way.

He clasped her tightly against him.

Then he lifted her into his arms, kissing her mouth as he strode for the bedroom doors.

She ran her fingers over his chest, reveling in the sparse, soft hair, palming his flat nipples, wondering if she was making him feel the same sensations.

He moaned her name one more time as he shakily set her on her feet next to the bed. Then he pulled her against his bare chest for another long kiss.

She flicked the single button at the side of the dress, and the fabric pooled around her ankles.

His hands stroked down her bare back, grasping her buttocks and pulling her hard against him.

She trembled a little at the thought of what would come next. But she was doing it. There was no power on earth that could stop her.

"Amanda?" he questioned, drawing back, gazing at her in the darkened room.

She pushed off his shirt, avoiding eye contact.

"You nervous?"

"No," she lied.

He paused. "You ever…"

This time she did look at him. No point in lying. He was going to figure it out soon anyway. She slowly shook her head. "Sorry."

He swore softly. Then his grip loosened. "Sorry?" He coughed. "You have just…" He tenderly kissed her mouth, then her cheeks, then her eyelids and her temples, drawing sensation after exquisite sensation up from her soul.

"If you're sure," he finally whispered.

"I am so sure," she breathed.

A smile formed on his lips and he traced his fingertip down her abdomen, dipping into her navel, over the downy curls, then he feathered a whisper-light touch on her tender flesh.

Her eyes went wide, and her jaw dropped open.

"You like?" he asked, his eyes burning into hers.

"Oh, yes."

His touch grew firmer, delved deeper.

She grasped his shoulders. "What should I do?"

"Nothing," he whispered.

"But—"

"You can't get it wrong, Mandy. There is absolutely no way for you to get this wrong."

Her muscles clenched and her eyes grew moist.

He gently laid her back on the bed, knees bent, feet still on the plush carpet.

"You tell me if I hurt you."

"You're not hurting me." He was so far from hurting her.

He left her for a second, kicking off his pants. But then he was back, and his hands were everywhere. She wanted time to stand still while she absorbed every possible sensation.

She took a deep breath, wanting to give back, wanting to make sure he was feeling half of what she was. She skimmed his chest with her knuckles, working her way lower across his taut skin. His abs contracted under her touch, and he gasped in her ear.

He groaned and kissed her mouth. She kissed him back, dueling with his tongue, arching into his touch, begging him with her body to go harder and deeper.

She wrapped her hand around him, and his heat seared her palm.

He swore, and she immediately jerked back.

"Did I hurt you?"

"You're killing me, babe."

"Sorry."

He gave a hollow laugh. "Kill me some more."

She did.

He shifted on top of her, his face showing the strains of control. "It's now or never."

She shifted her thighs to accommodate him. "Now," she said with conviction.

He pushed inside her in one swift stroke.

Her eyes widened with the pain, but he kissed it all away.

"It's going to be okay," he whispered in her ear.

It was already okay. The pain was fleeting, but the passion kept on.

He moved inside her, and her need blasted off. A driving pulse pounded in her thighs, her abdomen, her breasts.

As his pace increased, she kissed him hard, opening her body, her muscles stretching and tensing, reaching for something she couldn't identify.

Lightning burned behind her eyes. Electricity buzzed along her legs and a hot pool of sensation spread out from where their bodies joined.

He gasped her name, his entire body tensing as the world stood still for a microsecond.

Then relief pulsed through her, washing over her like summer rain, while the pounding pulse contracted her muscles and the lightning turned to streaks of color.

"Mrs. Elliott?"

A voice reached into her private thoughts. The limo driver.

She shook herself, her hand going to her chest as if to shield herself from the embarrassment of having been caught fantasizing about Daniel. "Uh, yes?"

He nodded to the brownstone building on the right. "We're here."

"Of course." Amanda moved shakily toward the limo door. "I'll be right there."

She allowed him to help her from the back seat, thanked him and crossed the sidewalk to her front door, where she carefully inserted the key.

Still, the memories of that prom night refused to fade.

She and Daniel had made magical love all night long. They'd said a bittersweet goodbye the next morning, knowing they would probably never see each other again.

And they wouldn't have. She'd have gone to NYU, and he'd have trekked all over the world.

If not for Bryan.

Bryan had changed everything.

Six

Daniel pulled his silver Lexus to the curb in front of the courthouse, determined to change tactics. He should have known his impulsive plan with Taylor wouldn't work on a woman as smart as Amanda.

But this time, things would be different.

He was slowing down, going on an intelligence-gathering mission. By the time he made his next move, she wouldn't even see it coming.

He set the emergency brake and shut off the engine. First things first. It was easy for him to see what should draw her to corporate law. It was harder for him to understand what drew her to criminal law.

But that was about to change.

He opened the driver's door and stepped out of the car. Amanda's receptionist—bless the woman's unthinking friendliness—had told Daniel exactly where to find Amanda. She was arguing an embezzlement case.

Embezzlement.

Employees stealing from their employers.

He slammed the car door shut and clamped his jaw. It was a glamorous career his ex-wife had chosen.

He glanced at his watch as he trotted up the wide, concrete steps. They were nearly an hour into the trial.

He pulled open the heavy oak doors, crossed the wide foyer and located courtroom number five.

There he quietly slipped into the back row.

The opposing lawyer was conducting the questioning, but Daniel could see the back of Amanda's head. She sat at the defendant's table next to a thin woman in a tan blouse with straight, mousy brown hair.

"Can you identify the signature on the check, Mr. Burnside?" the other lawyer asked the witness.

The witness looked up from a plastic sheaf in his hand and nodded toward the defendant. "It's Mary Robinson's signature."

"Did she have signing authority?" asked the lawyer.

The witness nodded. "For petty cash, office supplies, things like that."

"But she wouldn't normally write a check payable to herself?"

"Absolutely not," said the witness. "That's fraud."

Amanda stood up. "Objection, Your Honor. Speculation."

"Sustained," said the judge. He looked at the witness. "Just answer the questions."

The witness's mouth thinned.

"Can you tell us the amount of the check?" asked the lawyer.

"Three thousand dollars," the witness answered, eyes hard.

"Mr. Burnside, to the best of your knowledge, did Mary Robinson purchase office supplies with that three-thousand dollars?"

"She stole it," spat the witness.

Amanda stood again. "Your Honor—"

"Sustained," said the judge, wearily.

"But she did," Mr. Burnside insisted.

The judge looked down at him. "Are you arguing with me?"

He clamped his jaw.

"No further questions," said the lawyer.

Good move, thought Daniel. Burnside didn't seem to be helping the cause.

The judge looked to Amanda.

"No questions," she said.

"The prosecution rests," said the other lawyer.

"Ms. Elliott," said the judge, "you may call your first witness."

Amanda stood up. "The defense would like to call Collin Radaski to the stand."

A man in a dark suit stood up and made his way toward the aisle. Amanda turned to watch, and Daniel ducked behind a woman two rows up who was wearing a broad hat.

The bailiff swore in the witness, and Amanda approached the stand.

"Mr. Radaski, would you state your position at Westlake Construction Company."

Radaski leaned toward the microphone. "I'm the office manager."

"As part of your duties, do you approve payroll checks?"

He leaned in again. "Yes, I do."

Amanda walked back to the defendant's table and picked up a piece of paper. "Is it true, Mr. Radaski, that Jack Burnside instructed you to hold back holiday pay on those checks?"

"We don't include holiday pay every month."

"Is it also true that overtime was paid to Westlake Construction employees at straight time rather than time and a half?"

"We have a verbal agreement with employees regarding overtime."

Amanda raised her eyebrows and paused, making her disbelief known without saying a word. "A verbal agreement?"

"Yes, ma'am."

Amanda returned to the table and switched papers. "Are you aware, Mr. Radaski, that Westlake Construction has been breaking labor laws for over ten years?"

"What does that have to do with—"

"I object," called the prosecuting lawyer.

"On what grounds?" asked the judge.

"The witness is not in a position—"

"The witness is the office manager responsible for payroll," Amanda pointed out.

"Overruled," said the judge, and Daniel couldn't help a small smile of pride.

Amanda flipped through her notes.

Daniel was pretty sure it was all for show. The set of her shoulders told him she wasn't refreshing her memory. She knew exactly where she was going.

She looked up again. "Are you further aware, Mr. Radaski, that Westlake Construction owes my client four thousand, two hundred and eighty-six dollars in back overtime and holiday pay?"

"We had a verbal agreement," the witness sputtered.

"A verbal agreement of that nature has no force under New York labor law. Mr. Radaski, according to the accounting firm of Smith and Stafford, Westlake Construction owes current and former employees a total of one hundred and seventy-one thousand, six hundred and sixty-one dollars in back pay."

Radaski blinked at Amanda.

"Your Honor," she said, lifting a thick sheaf of papers from the table. "I would like to enter this actuarial report as exhibit D. My client wishes, at this time, to launch a countercomplaint against Westlake Construction for a settlement in the amount of one thousand, two hundred and eighty-six dollars, being the balance owed to her for unpaid overtime and holidays."

"But she stole three thousand dollars," shouted Jack Burnside from the galley.

The judge pounded his gavel.

Amanda's lips quirked in a small smile. "I'll be contacting current and former employees to ascertain their interest in a class action lawsuit."

The judge gazed at the prosecuting lawyer.

"I'd like to request a recess to confer with my client."

"I guess you would," said the judge. He brought the gavel down once again. "This case is adjourned until three o'clock Thursday afternoon."

Daniel quickly slipped out the door of the courtroom.

Okay, he could see the appeal. But surely those Perry Mason moments were few and far between.

Still, she was good.

Amanda stared at the small cardboard card that had accompanied a bouquet of twenty-four red roses.

Congratulations!

Puzzled, she flipped it over.

Saw you in court today. If I ever take up bank robbing, you'll be the first person I call.
—D

Daniel.

"Mr. Delectable?" asked Julie, breezing through the door with a stack of files.

"They're from Daniel," Amanda confirmed.

Julie leaned over to smell the roses. "This time you definitely have to do him on the desktop."

Amanda smiled at Julie's irreverence. "Daniel's not that kind of guy."

Julie toyed with the looped chain of her black choker. "It's a proven fact, sending red roses to an office means a guy wants to do it on the desktop."

"Where do you get these facts?"

"Didn't you read last month's *Cosmo?*"

Amanda cleared a space on the credenza for the flowers. "Afraid I missed it."

"I'll get you my copy."

Amanda set down the vase. "What do yellow roses mean?"

"Huh?"

"If a guy sends yellow roses to an office, what does that mean?"

Julie grinned. "Yellow means they want to do it on the desktop. Come to think of it, breathing means they want to do it on the desktop."

"Not Daniel." Amanda couldn't imagine any possible circumstances under which Daniel would make love on a desktop. It would be sacrilegious.

"Try him," Julie advised with a waggle of her dark eyebrows. "You'll be surprised."

"Daniel's not a surprise kind of guy."

"Were you expecting the roses?"

Amanda paused. "Nope. I have to admit, those were a surprise."

"There you go," said Julie.

"He's my ex." Amanda wasn't doing Daniel on the desktop or anywhere else. Bad enough that she'd kissed him.

"But he's hot."

He was hot all right, And he was still a fabulous kisser. And, unless she'd lost her mind, he'd responded to her kiss.

Which meant he was interested, too. Which meant they were both in big trouble.

"Amanda?"

Amanda blinked. "Hmm?"

Julie grinned. "You think he's hot, too."

"I think I'm late for a meeting."

A visit with Karen wasn't exactly a meeting, but as soon as Amanda walked out onto the veranda at The Tides, she was glad she'd come.

Karen was sitting on a deck chair with albums and photographs scattered around her.

"There you are," said Karen, pulling a brochure out of the mess. "I couldn't decide between a pedicure and reflexology."

"What are you doing?"

"I got us into Eduardo's for the twenty-fifth, but we should book our appointments early. You want a facial?"

"Sure," said Amanda, sitting in one of the other chairs. Now that she'd decided to do the spa weekend, she was getting a little excited about it.

Karen gestured to a pitcher of iced tea on a side table. "Thirsty?"

Amanda stood up again. "I'd love some. You want a refill?"

"Please." Karen put down the brochure and sat back in the padded chair. "Tell me about the world."

"The *entire* world?"

"Your world."

Amanda filled Karen's tall glass. "I won a case this morning."

"Congratulations."

"It's not exactly official yet. The judge will rule on Thursday, but I threatened Westlake Construction with a class action suit. They'll cave."

"Was that the Mary something embezzlement trial?"

Amanda nodded. "Sweet woman. Single mom, three kids. Nobody's served by her going to jail for six months."

"But she stole some money, right?"

Amanda sat down again. "She provided herself with an advance on holiday pay owed."

Karen grinned. "Will you be my lawyer?"

"You don't need a lawyer."

"I might. I'm bored. I'm thinking of taking up bank robbing."

"You been talking to Daniel?"

Karen's eyes sparkled. "No, have you?"

Amanda instantly regretted the impulsive joke. But backing off would only make Karen press harder.

"He sent me flowers," Amanda admitted. "He mentioned bank robbing, too. Is there something about the Elliott fortune you're not telling me?"

"What kind of flowers?"

"Roses."

"Red?"

"Yes."

"Holy cow."

"It's not what you think." Not that Amanda had any clue as to what she was supposed to think.

"How can it not be what I think?" asked Karen. "A dozen?"

Amanda hesitated. "Two."

"Two dozen red roses."

"They were congratulatory."

"Congratulatory for what?" Her eyes went wide. "What did you two do?"

Amanda quickly waved off the question. "It's nothing like that. He came to watch me in court. I won the case. He sent flowers."

Karen straightened one of the albums in front of her. "Daniel watched you in court?"

Amanda nodded.

"What for?"

"Beats me." She took a sip of the iced tea. "And, I tell you, he's making me nervous again. After the Taylor Hopkins thing, he said he was going to back off."

"What Taylor Hopkins thing?"

"Daniel invited Taylor to dinner, and Taylor gave me an indoctrination into the cult of the almighty dollar."

"Well, Taylor's definitely the guy to do it," said Karen. "Have you seen his new house?"

"Nope."

Karen sat forward and flipped a couple of pages in one of the albums. "Here it is."

Amanda stood up, coming around beside Karen. "Nice."

"It's on the shore. Fantastic tennis courts."

It was a nice house. But Amanda had never been overly impressed with expensive real estate. She glanced at the pictures of the extended Elliott Family. "What a wonderful picture of Scarlet and Summer."

"That was taken last year. Somehow we all ended up at Martha's Vineyard. Bridget went wild with the camera."

"Who's that with Gannon?"

"His date. I can't even remember her name. It was between rounds with Erika."

The mention of Erika reminded Karen of Gannon's recent wedding. "You have wedding pictures?"

"I sure do." Karen switched albums, opening to a formal shot of the bride and groom.

"Gorgeous dress," Amanda commented.

"She's a wonderful woman," said Karen. "So good for Gannon."

On the next page was a family shot. Amanda's gaze stopped on Daniel. He looked magnificent in a tux.

Then she saw the woman standing next to him.

"Oops," said Karen. "Sharon showed up. Nobody quite knew what to do about that."

Amanda squinted at her ex's ex. Sharon was petite and thin, with sculpted blond hair an expensive shade of platinum. She looked younger than forty. Her makeup was perfect, and her dress fairly dripped with silver sequins. The spray of flowers in her hair made her a competitor for the bride.

"I'm nothing like her, am I?" asked Amanda, suddenly overtaken by a wave of inadequacy.

"You're nothing like her," said Karen. "Thank goodness."

"But she's what Daniel wants."

Karen turned to gaze at Amanda. "You do know he divorced her."

"But he married her."

"He loved *you*."

Amanda shook her head. "I was pregnant."

Karen squeezed Amanda's arm. "You are a kind, compassionate, intelligent, loving—"

"And she's thin and beautiful, with a flair for designer clothes and multilingual small talk."

"She's cruel and brittle."

"But she looks great in an evening gown." There was no disputing that.

"So do you."

Amanda smiled. "You haven't seen me in an evening gown for more than a decade. Heck, I haven't seen myself in an evening gown for years."

"Maybe it's about time you did."

"I wear underwires," Amanda confessed in a whisper.

Karen chuckled. "Well, at least I don't need those anymore."

Amanda froze in horror.

But Karen shook her head. "Thank you so much. That was my first breast joke."

Amanda cringed. "But I—"

"Don't you dare apologize. You don't care about perfection. You blithely brought up breasts because you've forgotten all about my surgery."

It was true. When Amanda thought about Karen she didn't think of a double mastectomy; all she thought about was her true and wonderful friend.

"That's why I love you so dearly," said Karen, squeezing Amanda's arm. "Physical imperfections mean nothing to you."

Amanda glanced back down at Sharon. "They obviously mean something to Daniel." That was why he'd complained about Amanda's clothes and hair.

"I don't think that's true."

"We both agree that Sharon has nothing going for her except her appearance."

"Yeah," said Karen slowly.

"Then that's what attracted Daniel." Amanda glanced involuntarily at her plain navy pants and her white blouse.

"Do you care what he thinks?" asked Karen.

Good question. Amanda shouldn't care. She didn't want to be attractive to Daniel. She only wanted Daniel out of her life.

Still, the kiss, the flowers, her memories... Something was happening here. And she didn't know how to fight it.

"Dad?" Cullen bumped Daniel under the boardroom table and slipped him a sheet of paper.

Daniel snapped himself back to reality and focused on the expectant faces of the senior management team of Elliott Publication Holdings. He'd been wondering if Amanda liked the roses.

Stalling, he glanced down at the paper from Cullen.

Say: Cullen has those figures,

it read.

Daniel looked up, leaning back slightly in his chair. "Cullen has those figures."

Attention immediately swung to Cullen.

"The Spanish and German numbers look promising," said Cullen. "French is marginal, and translation costs for Japan make it a nonstarter."

Ah, the translation offices. Daniel knew what they were talking about now.

Daniel's brother Michael nodded. "We found pretty much the same results for *Pulse.* I'd want to talk about French, giving low shipping costs to Quebec and some domestic potential. But Japan will definitely give us diminishing returns."

Daniel's sister, Finola, spoke up. "*Charisma* is ready for any market."

"That's because you're image focused," said Michael. "You could probably sell without doing any translation at all."

"Still," said Finola, "it's part of the mix."

"What about you, Shane?" asked Michael.

Attention moved to Finola's twin brother, and Daniel knew everyone was wondering if Shane would take the perspective of his magazine or back up his twin.

"*The Buzz* could go either way," he said.

"Why don't we shelve the Japan discussion for today?" Cullen suggested.

"How does that help?" asked Cade McMann, the executive editor of *Charisma.* "Nothing's going to change."

"What if we prototype two translation offices," Cullen suggested. "Spanish and German. We're unlikely to lose on either of them, and it might answer some of the outstanding questions."

The room went silent as everybody considered the idea.

Cullen gave a small smile. "I don't think anyone wants to incur unnecessary losses this year, do they?"

There were nods all around on that.

"I can run it by Dad," Michael offered.

"Works for me," said Daniel, proud of his son's straightforward compromise.

"Then it's done," said Shane, smacking his hand on the table. "Can we adjourn? I've got a lunch meeting."

Everyone began gathering their papers and rising from their chairs.

Daniel pictured Amanda's smile one more time. He hoped she liked the roses. Maybe he'd call and ask—just to make sure they'd arrived.

"So much for the international advantage," said Cade as he and Finola paused behind Daniel's chair.

"I knew they'd vote Japan down anyway," Finola answered.

"Did you give any more thought to my concerns about Jessie Clayton?" asked Cade.

"My intern?"

"Yeah."

"I don't have an opinion. I've barely seen her. You know, it's almost like she's avoiding me."

"But why?" asked Cade.

"Who knows." Finola laughed. "Maybe I'm scary."

"I don't trust her."

"Then do some digging."

"Maybe I will." Cade's voice trailed off as they moved toward the exit.

"Got a minute, Dad?" asked Cullen as Daniel started to rise.

Daniel sat back down. "Sure."

The boardroom door closed on the rest of the management team, and they were alone.

Cullen pivoted his chair and leaned back, rolling a gold pen between his fingertips. "Okay, what's going on?"

"What do you mean?"

Cullen scoffed and shook his head. "I mean, I had to save your ass three times in that meeting. What's got you so distracted?"

"You didn't—"

Cullen tapped his finger on the note he'd passed Daniel.

"I was a little distracted."

"A *little?*"

"I was just wondering—"

"About Mom."

"About business."

"Yeah, yeah. It was the potential French market that put that twinkle in your eyes."

"I didn't have a twinkle."

Cullen set down his pen, suddenly looking every inch the senior executive. "What are you doing, Dad?"

Daniel searched his son's expression. "About what?"

"You went to her court case yesterday."

"So? I'm trying to get her to change professions. You know that."

Cullen shook his head, giving Daniel a sly smile. "Dad, Dad, Dad."

Daniel raised his eyebrows. "What, what, what?"

"Admit it."

"Admit what?"

"You've got the hots for Mom."

Daniel nearly choked. "What?"

"This isn't about her job."

Daniel didn't answer. He rocked back in his chair and stared incredulously at his son.

Cullen didn't know about the kiss. He couldn't know about the kiss. Even the Elliott grapevine wasn't that efficient.

Cullen straightened in his chair. "Dad, I talked—"

"To *whom?*"

"To Bryan. We both think it's a good idea."

"You think what's a good idea?" Him kissing Amanda, Amanda kissing him?

"You and Mom getting back together."

Daniel held up his hands. "Whoa."

"You might have a hard time convincing her—"

"Your confidence in me is inspiring."

"But we think it'll be worth it."

"Oh, you do, do you?"

"Absolutely."

Daniel leaned forward and stared hard at his youngest son. He didn't know what was going on between himself and Amanda, but whatever it was, he sure didn't need a misguided cheering section.

"Back off," he ordered tersely.

"Now, Dad—"

"I mean it, Cullen."

"I don't care what you mean. It's time to move past that corporate law stuff."

"No way." Daniel wasn't giving up.

"It's a ruse, anyway. Just go ahead and date her."

"She's not—"

"Send her flowers or something."

"I already—" Daniel snapped his mouth shut.

"You already what?"

Daniel jumped to his feet and scooped up his files. "This meeting is over."

Cullen stood, too. "You already what?"

"You're an impudent young punk."

"She hasn't had a boyfriend for a while."

That stopped Daniel. "What do you mean 'for a while'?" The thought of Amanda dating someone else sent a spear through Daniel's chest. It was the same reaction he'd had when Taylor had flirted with her.

"Roberto somebody or other proposed last Christmas."

"Proposed?"

"She said no. But I think you have a better chance."

Somebody else had proposed to Amanda? Another man had *proposed* to his wife?

The breath went out of Daniel's lungs. She could have said yes. She could have been married by now—out of reach, out of touch. And he wouldn't have had the chance...

To what?

What was he thinking here?

Cullen's palms came down on the tabletop. "Take her out on the town. Make her feel special."

Daniel stared blankly at his son.

"She likes lobster," said Cullen.

Hoffman's did a great lobster. Or Angelico's. Daniel pictured Amanda across the table from him in a softly lit restaurant.

She looked good.

She looked *really* good.

With a sinking certainty, Daniel knew his son was right. And that meant Daniel was in big trouble. He wanted to date his ex-wife.

Seven

Daniel had been on a hundred dates, maybe a thousand. He knew impressions mattered. And he knew enough to focus on the details. First thing he needed here was a skilled calligrapher and a single white rose.

There was a little print shop down on Washington Square that would do an elegant invitation and do it quickly. He could have the driver drop it all off at Amanda's later this afternoon.

He rocked back in his chair and buzzed Nancy.

Two hours later, he had his answer.

In an e-mail from Amanda.

An *e-mail* of all things.

He'd gone for style and elegance, and she'd chosen expediency.

He double clicked her name.

No, thanks, the message said. Could she have been any more terse and impersonal?

This gave him nothing. No explanation. No room to re-schedule. Nothing.

No thanks? He didn't think so. He hadn't brought *Snap* magazine this far by taking "no thanks" for an answer.

He hit the buzzer. "Nancy?"

"Yes?"

"Get me Amanda Elliott's office, please."

"Right away," said Nancy.

When the light on line one blinked, he picked up again. "Amanda?"

"It's Julie."

"Oh. Is Amanda available? It's Daniel Elliott calling."

"Mr. Delectable?" asked Julie.

"Excuse me?"

She giggled. "One moment, please."

Daniel rubbed his temple, taking a deep breath. He didn't want a fight. He just wanted a date. A simple dinner and some conversation so he could find out where things stood between them.

Her husky voice came on the line. "Amanda Elliott."

"Amanda? It's Daniel."

Silence.

"I got your e-mail." He kept his voice even and nonjudg-mental.

"Daniel—"

He played dumb. "Is Friday night bad for you?"

There was a pause. "It's not a scheduling problem."

"Really?" He leaned back in his leather chair. "What kind of a problem is it?"

"Don't do this, Daniel."

"Don't do what?"

"The roses were great. But—"

"But, what?"

"Okay." She paused. "Honestly?"

"Of course."

She drew a breath. "I don't have the energy."

He straightened his chair with a snap. "I take *energy?*" How did he take energy?

"Daniel." Exasperation built in her voice.

"*I'll* make the reservation. *I'll* pick you up. *I'll* pay the bill and *I'll* bring you home. How does that take energy?"

"It's not the travel arrangements that take energy."

"What is it, then?"

"It's you. You take energy. You said you'd back off, but then you came to the courthouse."

"I will back off. I *am* backing off."

"Yeah, right," she scoffed. "Spying on me is backing off."

"I wasn't spying." Well, maybe he was. But that was yesterday. Now he had a different mission. A better mission.

"You watched me in court."

"So did several other members of the public."

"Daniel."

It was time to go for broke, time to pull out all the stops. "You were right, and I was wrong, and I'll stop."

There was a long silence.

Then there was a hint of a smile in her tone. "Could you repeat that?"

He snorted. "I don't think so."

Another silence.

"What's the catch?"

He swiveled his chair, loving the breathy sound of her voice. "No catch. I'd like to take you to dinner. My way of apologizing."

"Apologizing? You?"

"Yes. I think we've made some good progress in our relationship, Mandy."

She inhaled sharply at the sound of her nickname.

"And I don't want to lose that," he continued. "And I

promise I will not venture an opinion on either criminal or corporate law for the duration of dinner."

There was a smile in her voice. "Will anyone join us at the last minute?"

"Not if I can help it."

"What does that mean?"

He couldn't remember doing quite this much work to get a date before. He must be slipping.

"It means," he said, "that while I cannot vouch for the behavior of all the citizens of New York City, I have not invited, nor will I invite, anyone else to join us."

"Is that a promise?"

"I swear."

Another silence. "Okay."

"Friday night?"

"Friday night."

"I'll pick you up at eight."

"Goodbye, Daniel."

"Goodbye, Amanda." Daniel grinned, holding his hand against the receiver for an extra minute as he hung up the phone. He'd done it.

Now all he needed was a pound of Soleil Gold chocolates and a reservation at Hoffman's.

Amanda was definitely underdressed for Hoffman's. She'd rushed home from the office and thrown on a black denim skirt and a cropped cotton blouse. Her makeup was light, and her hair was combed back behind her ears, showing off simple jade earrings. She'd suggested popping down to the bistro at the corner for a steak sandwich, but Daniel wouldn't be budged.

In true Elliott fashion, he'd wrangled reservations to the "it" place and was preparing to show off his money and his connections.

She didn't know who he was trying to impress. Fifty-dollar appetizers didn't do a thing for her. And she sure wasn't a trophy to flash in the faces of his society cohorts.

A tuxedo-clad waiter tucked them into a softly lit alcove, next to a bay window overlooking the park. Daniel ordered them each a martini.

Okay, she'd admit the high-backed, silk-upholstered chairs were comfortable. And the expensive art, fine china and antique furnishings were easy on the eyes.

The waiter laid a linen napkin across her lap and handed Daniel a leather-bound wine list. Since Elliotts measured the importance of an occasion in dollars, she knew something had to be going on here.

She leaned forward. "You swear this isn't part of some grand plan to coerce me into changing careers?"

"So cynical," said Daniel with a disarming grin.

"So experienced," said Amanda, watching his expression carefully. She half expected Taylor Hopkins to jump out from behind a Jacobean cabinet.

Daniel let the wine list fall open in his hands, scanning the first page. "You should relax and enjoy dinner."

"I will," she said. "As soon as the ah-ha moment is over."

He glanced up. "The ah-ha moment?"

"The moment when that final, significant piece of evidence is revealed, and all of this makes sense."

"You spend too much time in a courtroom."

"I spent too much time married to you."

Daniel closed the menu and gazed at her over the low candle. "Okay. Let me see if I can move things along here."

That surprised her. "You're going to 'fess up to the nefarious plot?"

A busboy in a short red jacket stopped to fill their water glasses and place a basket of fresh rolls on the table.

Daniel thanked him, then returned his attention to Amanda. "There is no nefarious plot. Bryan's the covert operator, not me."

"Ha. Everything he knows he learned from his dad."

"Everything he knows he learned from the CIA."

Amanda flinched.

Daniel reached for her hand, squeezing her fingers and sending a warm buzz up her arm. "Sorry."

She shook her head. "It's all right. It's over. That's what counts."

"It's over," Daniel agreed.

Amanda drew a breath, retrieving her hand. "Okay, confess. What's going on?"

"I wanted to tell you I thought you were terrific in the courtroom."

The compliment gave her a warm glow, but she fought the feeling. This was no time to go all soft over Daniel. He was still up to something.

"That's nice. But that's not why we're here," she pointed out, reaching for a roll. They were warm and fragrant, one of her biggest weaknesses in life.

"We're here because I realized when I watched you nail that guy that I was wrong to push you to change careers."

There was no ignoring that compliment. It wasn't glib, and it wasn't generic, and she knew deep down in her soul that it was sincere.

The waiter appeared and set a martini in front of each of them. "Are you ready to order?" he asked, stepping back.

"Give us a few minutes," said Daniel, his gaze never leaving Amanda.

The waiter inclined his head and withdrew.

Daniel picked up his martini glass to salute her.

Amanda lifted her own glass. "Let's say I believe you."

"I'd applaud your intelligence."

"But I still think you're up to something."

He shrugged. "What you see is what you get."

"Yeah, right. The Elliotts are known far and wide for their transparency."

He slowly focused his attention, his intense gaze thickening the air between them. "I'm being as transparent as I know how."

She waited.

"Think about it, Amanda. Candy, flowers, dinner…"

She blinked. "We're on a *date?*"

His smile held a hint of pride. "We're on a date."

She waved her silver butter knife. "No, we're not. You're apologizing. We're getting our relationship back on an even keel, for the sake of our children and our grandchildren."

Daniel shrugged in a way that emphasized his broad shoulders. "Whatever you say. I'm not going to argue with you, Amanda."

She stared at him in mutinous silence.

The waiter appeared at Daniel's elbow. "Are you ready to order?"

"Yes. Thank you." Daniel glanced at Amanda. "The lobster?"

The fact that he remembered her favorite meal gave her a little thrill. But she squelched it. This wasn't a date. He wasn't her boyfriend. Those stupid intimate details were just old habits.

"The scallops," she said, to be contrary, handing the waiter the menu. "And a garden salad."

Daniel's eyebrows quirked. "You're sure?"

She nodded.

"I'll have the scallops, as well," he said.

"But—"

He shot her a silent question.

"Nothing." She'd expected him to order a rib eye, but she wasn't about to admit that.

As a harpist began playing in the far corner, Amanda smoothed the napkin over her lap and regrouped. Tonight was about maintaining an even keel.

She searched her mind for a neutral topic. "So, uh, did you get your legal troubles solved?"

Daniel took a sip of his martini. "What legal troubles?"

"The employee manual."

"Ahhh." He nodded. "Those legal troubles. Unfortunately, it looks like we're going to have to fire the man."

"You're going to fire someone over the employee manual?"

"Afraid so."

An instant defensiveness bubbled up inside her. "You're pretty cavalier with someone's livelihood."

"Well, he was pretty cavalier with his job."

"What did he do?"

"Time theft."

"What's time theft?"

"When you're doing personal business on company time."

"What? Like making a hair appointment?"

Daniel gave a hard sigh. "You don't fire someone over a hair appointment."

"I don't, but it sounds like you might."

"He called in sick and then was spotted on Seventh Avenue by one of the managers."

"Maybe he was picking up a prescription."

"According to my sources, he looked hale and hearty."

Her eyebrows went up. "You have *sources?* Bryan really does get it from you."

Daniel stroked his fingers along the stem of his martini glass. "Even you have to admit that a company the size of EPH can't afford to have employees abusing sick leave."

Amanda didn't have to admit any such thing. "Did you ask the guy what happened?"

"Not personally."

"Did anyone ask him what happened?"

"He was offered a chance to bring in a doctor's note. He didn't take it."

Amanda leaned across the table. "Maybe he didn't see a doctor."

Daniel took another swig of his martini. "He signed for sick leave. He wasn't sick. That's fraud."

"Did he get a fair and impartial hearing?"

"Why? You want to take on the case?"

She met his level gaze with a challenging smile. "I'd love to take on the case."

Daniel pushed back his chair. "We should dance."

"Excuse me?"

He nodded to a staircase. "There's dancing on the veranda upstairs."

"But we just ordered."

He stood and held out his hand. "I'll get them to hold it. I think we should do something that doesn't require talking for a while."

Amanda opened her eyes wide and feigned innocence. "Am I ruining your perfect date?"

"Let's just say you're a bigger challenge than most."

"Maybe you should dump me."

"I'm a gentleman."

Amanda stood up without taking his hand. "Really, Daniel. You could cancel our order and take me home."

She tensed, waiting for his answer.

Getting out of here would be the smart thing to do. The safe thing to do. Dancing with him would be the stupid and dangerous thing to do.

"Don't be ridiculous." He captured her hand, and she hated the feeling of relief.

His fingers were warm and strong as they twined with hers, and the resistance evaporated from her body.

"This isn't a date," she affirmed as he led her toward the worn, wood staircase.

"Of course it's a date. I sent you roses."

"You know, my entire house smells like a florist."

He gestured for her to go first up the narrow staircase. "This is a bad thing?"

"It's a weird thing."

"Your old boyfriends didn't send you flowers?"

She twisted her head to look at him. "What old boyfriends?"

"Cullen told me about Roberto."

She tripped on a stair and grabbed for the handrail. Roberto had been intense, too passionate. She didn't need to save the *entire* world. She was just going for one small corner.

Daniel's hands closed on her waist to steady her. "I hear he proposed."

She regained her balance. "He did."

"You said no?"

"I did."

"Why?"

"None of your business." She pushed open a heavy door at the top of the stairs and the sound of a string quartet wafted over her.

Daniel reached over her head and took the weight of the door. "Fair enough."

Amanda had expected an argument so his words took her by surprise.

He put a hand on the small of her back and guided her onto the open-air dance floor.

She immediately realized dancing with him was a colossal mistake. But then, it was beginning to look as though this whole evening was a mistake. Amanda should have known better. When an Elliott pulled out all the stops, a woman was pretty much powerless to resist.

He drew her into his arms and she automatically matched his rhythm.

The evening breeze was cool. Even the stars were cooperating—shining brightly in an unusually clear sky. She wondered for a moment if the superrich could control the weather. Maybe there was a secret satellite network out there.

She tipped her head back and stared straight up at the scattering of silver flecks against midnight purple. "Is everything you do always so perfect?"

There was a chuckle deep in his throat. "So perfect?"

"Perfect flowers, perfect dinner, perfect sky."

He looked up with her. "All it takes is a little forethought and planning."

She tipped her head back down. "And you are the planner."

"I am the planner."

"Ever do anything without a plan?"

"Nope."

"Nothing?"

He shrugged. "What would be the point?"

The quartet segued into another waltz, and Daniel gathered her even closer. She shouldn't like this. Didn't want to like this. It was bad enough fantasizing about him when she was alone in the back of a limo. Fantasizing about him in his arms was downright dangerous.

"It might be fun," she said, forcing herself to keep the conversation going. Last thing she wanted was to give her sexy thoughts free rein.

"What's fun about disorganization?" he asked.

The wind gusted, blowing a strand of hair across her face. "I'm talking spontaneity."

He tucked the wayward hair behind her ear, his blunt fingertips brushing her cheek. "Spontaneity is just another word for chaos."

She shook the hair loose again. "Spontaneity is doing what you want when you want."

"That's just flighty."

"Are you calling me flighty?"

He touched his forehead to hers and sighed. "I'm not calling you anything. I'm just saying I don't change so much in a week that I want completely different things by the end of it."

"What about in a month, in a year?"

"There are different levels of planning."

Amanda drew back, her feet coming to a stop. "You actually have something planned for a year down the road?"

"Of course."

"No way."

"There's the annual budget cycle, reservations, conferences. You don't just hop on a plane to Paris and throw up an EPH display at the European Periodical League."

"But what if something changes?"

He pulled her back into the dance, stroking his warm palm along her spine and making her shiver. "What would change? I mean fundamentally?"

Despite her effort to keep up a good argument, her voice was growing softer, more sultry than the moist night air. "But don't you ever just want to live life on the fly?"

"No."

"Not even the little things?"

"Amanda." His voice went gravelly, and his hand continued its leisurely path up and down her spine. "There are no little things."

Now that was just plain crazy. "What about dinner? Wouldn't it have been fun to pick a restaurant on the spur of the moment?"

There was a chuckle in his voice as he danced them toward one of the outer railings. "You mean you'd have rather waited in line for two hours to get a table?"

Mustering her fading energy, she smacked her hand against his arm. "You're being deliberately obtuse."

"I'm being deliberately logical. Planning doesn't take the fun out of life. It keeps the fun *in* life because it takes out the worry."

She looked up at him again. "Get out on a limb once in a while."

"I don't think so."

"It'll make you feel alive."

He paused, brushing the wayward hair from her face again. This time her shiver was obvious.

"You think?" he asked softly.

"I know," she said with assurance.

"Okay. Here's something you probably didn't plan on."

Her interest perked up. "Yeah?"

He nodded, slowly drawing her toward him. "Yeah." He bent down, slanting his mouth.

Her eyes went wide. *Uh-oh.* There was spontaneity and then there was *spontaneity.*

"This," he whispered as his lips touched hers.

It was a gentle kiss. His lips barely parted, and the arm at her back eased rather than pulled her against his body.

It couldn't have lasted more than ten seconds, but a frenzy of desire thrummed to life inside her. The silver stars blurred inside her head and her knees went weak.

Then he opened his mouth, and the image melted. She clung to his shoulders, silently repeating his name over and over inside her head.

Just when her frenzied words threatened to break free, he ended the kiss.

They stared at each other, standing still amongst the swaying couples, breathing deeply for long minutes.

"Didn't plan on that, did you?" he finally asked.

She considered the glint in his eye. "Did *you?*"

"Oh, yeah. All week."

"What?"

He chuckled low. "I'm a planner, Amanda. That's just the way it is."

"But—"

"And I don't think my careful planning distracted from my enjoyment one little bit."

Amanda drew back. He'd planned to kiss her?

A frightening thought entered her head, and she tightened her grip on his arms to steady herself. "Please tell me you haven't got anything else planned."

His white teeth flashed in the lantern light. "It's probably better if I don't answer that."

Eight

Daniel's intercom buzzed on Monday morning, and Nancy's voice came through the speaker. "Mrs. Elliott to see you."

Amanda? Here?

Daniel could hardly believe it.

She'd seemed so jumpy after their kiss on Friday night, he'd decided to back off for a few days.

Maybe he'd been unwise to tip his hand. But he wanted to date her, and he wanted her to know that he was interested. The more he saw of her, the more he remembered what they had together, and the more he wanted to recapture the magic.

He stood up from his desk and straightened his tie, smoothing back his hair with one hand.

"Daniel?" came Nancy's voice again.

He pushed the intercom button. "Send her in."

The door opened and he put a welcoming smile on his face.

Then the smile died.

It was Sharon.

The *other* Mrs. Elliott.

She marched into his office, all five foot three of her, almost painfully thin with hair that had seen way too many salon treatments. Her blue eyes crackled as she swung the door behind her. It closed with a bang.

Daniel braced himself.

"I don't know what the hell you thought you were up to," she hissed, advancing on his desk.

"Up to?"

"Hoffman's?"

He dropped down into his chair and shuffled through a stack of papers. "Is there something I can help you with, Sharon?"

She paced in front of his desk. "Yes, there's something you can help me with. You can uphold the terms of our divorce agreement."

"You got this month's check." She'd cashed it within hours.

"I'm not talking about the money," she all but screeched. "I'm talking about our agreement."

"Our agreement to what?" Daniel signed the letter in front of him, then moved his attention to a marketing report. "I've got a busy morning here." And he didn't want to waste valuable brain space focused on Sharon when he could be daydreaming about Amanda. He wondered if she was busy for lunch.

Sharon placed both her hands on Daniel's desktop and leaned forward. It was hard for an overbleached pixie to look intimidating, but she was doing her best. "Our agreement to tell our friends *I* was the one who left *you*."

"I never told them any different."

"Actions speak louder than words, Daniel."

He glanced at his watch. "Can we skip to the point? I've got a ten o'clock with Michael."

Her jaw clenched, and her eyes wrinkled up despite two

very expensive surgeries. "Nobody's going to believe me if you're necking on the dance floor with some other woman."

Daniel squared his shoulders. "That wasn't another woman. It was Amanda."

Sharon waved a hand. "Whatever, you just—"

"And we weren't necking."

"Stay away from her, Daniel."

"No."

Sharon's pale blue eyes nearly popped out of her head. "*What?*"

He stood up and crossed his arms over his chest. "I said no."

"How dare—"

"I dare because you and I are divorced, and I will see whomever I want whenever I want."

"We had an agreement," she sputtered.

"I agreed to lie once to save your reputation. It's over. We're done. You have absolutely no say in my life anymore. Got that?" Particularly when it came to Amanda. Daniel wasn't taking direction from anyone ever again when it came to Amanda. Well, maybe Cullen. But that was only because Cullen was smart, and Daniel happened to agree with him on this.

Sharon put on a pretty pout, and her expression was almost magically transformed. It was embarrassing to think he'd once fallen for that trick.

"But, Daniel," she whined, "I'll be humiliated."

"Why?"

"Because people will think you dumped me."

"If you want to save your reputation, get your own dates. Go out. Be happy. Show them all you're well rid of me."

Crocodile tears welled up in her eyes. But Daniel was unmoved.

She'd made her bed, and it was up to her to lie in it. He'd given her the house, the artwork, the season tickets and the staff. He was done.

He moved out from behind the desk, heading for the door.

"You're on your own, Sharon. Fool them however you want, but leave me out of it."

"But, Daniel—"

"No. I'm through. We're done."

She straightened and squared her shoulders. "At least keep that woman out of the public eye."

Daniel clenched his jaw on the words he wanted to hurl at her. He opened the door. "Goodbye, Sharon."

She sniffed, put her pointed chin in the air, tucked her clutch purse under one arm and marched out.

Daniel shut the door firmly behind her and stalked back to his desk.

Keep Amanda out of the public eye?

He didn't think so.

He buzzed Nancy. "We have any high-profile invitations for this weekend? Something splashy, with the who's who?"

"He *kissed* you?" asked Karen, her green eyes lighting up with a grin as she tamped soil around an African violet.

She was working in the solarium, hand tools, potting soil and fertilizer scattered on the table in front of her.

"Am I crazy?" asked Amanda, carrying a tray of seedlings to a shelf on the other side of the sunlit room.

"Crazy to fall for your ex-husband?"

Amanda groaned as she walked back. "It sounds so much worse when you say it out loud."

"It doesn't sound bad at all. It's really very sweet," said Karen, stripping off her brightly colored gloves and sitting down heavily in a wicker chair.

Amanda quickly went to her. "You okay?"

Karen nodded and smiled. "Just a little tired. But it's a good kind of tired." Her gaze went to the plants. "It feels great to accomplish something."

Amanda crouched down and squeezed Karen's hand. "It feels great to see you so energetic."

"Back to you and Daniel."

Amanda groaned, but Karen just laughed.

A phone rang.

Then it rang again.

Karen glanced at Amanda's purse sitting next to the African violet. "Is your cell turned on?"

Amanda jumped up. "Oh, shoot. I'll shut it off."

"See who it is," said Karen.

Amanda flipped it open and checked the call display. Her chest contracted—not a good sign. "It's Daniel."

"Pick it up," Karen urged, sitting forward.

Amanda squeezed her eyes shut for a second then pushed the talk button.

"Amanda Elliott."

"Hey, Mandy. It's Daniel."

She felt her cheeks heat, and Karen grinned.

"Hi, Daniel."

"Listen, are you free on Saturday night?"

"Uh, Saturday?"

Karen nodded vigorously.

"Let me…" Amanda paused, not wanting to look too eager. She didn't know what they were doing, or where they were going, but she wanted to feel that rush of excitement one more time. "Saturday's fine."

"Good. There's a museum fund-raiser at the Riverside Ballroom."

The Riverside? As in the hotel where they'd first made love? Amanda opened her mouth, but nothing came out.

"Pick you up at eight?" asked Daniel.

"I… Uh…"

"It's black tie. For a really good cause."

Of course it was a good cause. Daniel always showed up

for the good cause. Just as he always showed up for the reporters and the movers and shakers.

Why couldn't they just go out for pizza?

"Amanda?" he prompted.

"Yeah?"

"Eight o'clock's okay?"

"Sure."

"Great. See you then."

Amanda closed her little phone.

"Another date?" asked Karen with a sly grin.

"The museum fund-raiser at the Riverside."

Karen's breath whistled out. "Now, that's a date."

"I have nothing to wear."

Karen waved a dismissive hand. "Sure you do."

Amanda tucked her phone back into her purse. "No,
really. I've been through my entire closet. I have absolutely
nothing to wear."

"Let's see if we can help you."

"How do you mean?"

Karen stood up. "Scarlet must have a hundred of her
designs upstairs."

Amanda took a step back. "I couldn't."

"Sure you could. It'll be fun." Karen took Amanda's arm.
"If it makes you feel better, we'll call her for permission
when we find something. But she's going to be thrilled."

Amanda allowed Karen to tug her toward the door. "You
think she'll let me wear her clothes?"

"Absolutely. And if we need alterations, we'll get her
over here."

Amanda hesitated. "I'm not—"

"Humor me on this," said Karen. "I'll feel like I'm going
to the party myself."

"You actually like that kind of thing?" Amanda asked as
they headed up the staircase.

"It's fun getting all dressed up."

"Well, that's the difference between you and me." Amanda felt stiff and plastic in formal wear, not to mention heavy makeup and hairspray. Her expression would go tight, and even her voice would go formal. She felt as if she was making people dig through layers to get to the real her.

"So, are you going to kiss him again?" asked Karen.

"I hadn't thought about it." Now that was a lie. She'd fantasized about kissing, kissing and more kissing in the days since Friday.

"Well *think* about it."

They entered one of the spare bedrooms, and Karen opened the double doors of a walk-in closet.

"Okay. I'm going to sit down here and get comfortable," she said. "And I want you to give me a fashion show and a monologue on kissing your ex-husband."

Amanda laughed. "It was a short kiss."

"But a good one?" asked Karen, easing down into an armchair and putting her feet on the matching ottoman.

Amanda let her mind go back for the thousandth time. "A good one," she agreed. A very good one. An "I think I remember why I married you" good one.

"You should see the expression on your face," Karen clucked.

"I just wish I could figure it out," Amanda called as she entered the closet. "I mean, we're divorced. We're living completely different lives."

"Maybe he's just after your body."

Amanda leaned back out the door. "Hello? After Sharon?"

"Especially after Sharon. That woman might look good in pictures, but believe me, up close it's all makeup, *Botox* and putty filler."

Amanda choked out a laugh.

Karen laughed along with her. "She's frightening, particularly when she starts talking. You, on the other hand, get more gorgeous by the minute."

Amanda didn't believe her, but Karen was a very kind friend.

"Now," said Karen, "we are going to knock that man dead with a sexy dress."

"I'm not sure I can pull off sexy," said Amanda.

"Don't be silly. You can do sexy with one hand behind your back."

Even if she could pull it off, she wouldn't. "If I go out there all vamped up, you know what he's going to think."

"What's he going to think?"

Amanda frowned at Karen. "That I'm…you know…interested in him."

"You *are* interested in him."

"Not as a boyfriend."

"As what then?"

Amanda peeled off her blouse. She sighed. "Isn't that the million-dollar question."

"He can be your clandestine lover," said Karen.

"A secret affair? With Daniel?"

"It's not like you've never slept with him before," Karen said.

Amanda rolled her eyes.

Karen laughed. "May I assume it was good?"

"Of course it was good." Amanda peeled off her pants and laid them on the bed. Sex had never been the issue in their marriage. The issues had been Daniel's overbearing family, his drive to make money and his unrelenting pretension.

In the early years, they'd had something real, and it had broken her heart to watch it slowly slip away as Daniel retreated further and further into the shell of propriety. But the sex, ah, the sex…

"So, the sex was good but the marriage went bad?" asked Karen.

Amanda stepped into the closet again. "That's one way of putting it."

"You could have the best of both worlds," Karen called. "Sleep with the good lover, but live apart from the bad husband."

"That's—" Amanda stopped. She walked back to the closet door and stared at Karen. It was either crazy, or a pretty good idea.

"It is the twenty-first century," said Karen.

Daniel as a lover, and only a lover?

He'd already promised to back off on the career advice, so she wouldn't have to endure any more lectures. Could she really take advantage of his strengths and simply ignore his weaknesses?

"You are going to need one special dress," said Karen with a knowing wink.

Amanda couldn't put her finger on it, but something about this just wasn't quite right.

"I couldn't…" she began.

"Actually," said Karen, "you could. It's not illegal, immoral or unhealthy."

The Elliotts' housekeeper appeared in the doorway. "Do you ladies need anything?"

"Yes, Olive. We need champagne and orange juice," said Karen decisively. "We're celebrating."

"Are you allowed?" asked Amanda.

"In moderation," said Karen.

"I'll bring it right up," said Olive, exiting the room.

Karen pointed imperiously to the closet. "I want you to start with the dresses you'd be least likely to wear in public."

Amanda strolled into the museum fund-raiser in a black sheath of oriental silk. Sleeveless, it had a mandarin collar that eliminated the need for jewelry, and it was slit up the back for easy walking. A floral silkscreen of gold and pink cascaded diagonally across the front.

One of Scarlet's designs, it was a compromise with Karen—elegant but not overly flirtatious.

Scarlet had insisted on a thin golden anklet that winked when Amanda walked and complemented her strappy sandals. The heels were higher than she normally wore, but Daniel gave her a steady arm to hang on to.

As they entered through an ornate archway, she took in flamboyant floral arrangements and chandeliers dripping with crystal teardrops. The ceiling beams were white with inlayed gold. Perimeter tables were immaculately set and a circular dance floor gleamed in the center of the room.

Cinderella's ball had nothing on this place.

Then she spotted Patrick and Maeve. Her stomach clenched and she stumbled a step. "You didn't tell me your parents were going to be here," she whispered to Daniel, feeling eighteen and impossibly gauche all over again.

"Is that a problem?" he whispered back.

"Yes, it's a problem," she hissed.

"Why?"

What a question. "Because they don't like me."

"Don't be ridiculous."

She slowed. The glitz, glitter and orchestra music were suddenly making her claustrophobic. She didn't belong here. She'd never belonged here.

She needed to proposition Daniel and get out.

"Daniel, darling." A sixtyish woman dripping in sequins and wearing enough diamonds to cancel the national debt gave Daniel a kiss on each cheek.

Daniel smiled and clasped her papery hand. "Mrs. Cavalli."

"I saw your mother at the Humane Society quilt raffle last week."

"I heard it went well," said Daniel with an easy interest.

"It did." Mrs. Cavalli's gaze strayed to Amanda.

Daniel put his hand on the small of her back. "This is my friend, Amanda. Amanda, Mrs. Cavalli."

Amanda held out her hand. "Pleased to meet you."

"Do you have any pets, dear?"

"Uh, no." Amanda shook her head. "I'm afraid I don't."

"You should consider adopting one from the shelter. That's where we got Buttons, three, maybe four years ago." Mrs. Cavalli turned to Daniel. "The little dickens got into some caramel candy last week."

"Did she?"

Mrs. Cavalli chuckled, her bosom jiggling. "Took the groomer three hours to get it out of her fur."

Then she turned back to Amanda. "She's a cockapoo. Big brown eyes. Just a treasure."

"She sounds adorable," said Amanda.

"Will we see you at the Children's Hospital tea, dear?"

Amanda glanced at Daniel.

"Amanda works during the day," he said.

Mrs. Cavalli drew back, her eyes rounding. "Oh, I see."

"Amanda is a lawyer."

"Well, that's lovely, dear. Perhaps another time?"

"Perhaps," said Amanda.

Mrs. Cavalli gave a fluttery-fingered wave. "I must go find Maeve."

"Nice to see you," called Daniel.

"Daniel!" boomed a hearty voice as a gray-haired man in a tuxedo reached for his hand.

"Senator Wallace," Daniel greeted in return.

"Did you catch the closing numbers in oil futures this afternoon?" asked Wallace.

Without waiting for an answer, he held up his palms. "We have *got* to drill in Alaska, that's all there is to it. Sooner the better as far as California is concerned."

"What about conservation measures?" asked Daniel.

Senator Wallace pointed his index finger at Daniel. "You show me an SUV owner willing to turn down his air-conditioning, and I'll show you a liberal Democrat about to support Adam Simpson." He laughed heartily.

Amanda smiled, even though she didn't really understand the joke.

"You get caught up in the Chesapeake scandal?" asked the senator.

Daniel shook his head. "I got out of tech stocks early."

"Damn accountants," said the senator. "No better than the lawyers."

Amanda's discomfort must have shown, because Senator Wallace acknowledged her for the first time. "Don't get me wrong, little lady. I'm a lawyer myself. But damn these upstarts, we've got to put the economic clout back in the hands of the Fortune 500."

Amanda clenched her jaw, and her hand tightened on Daniel's arm.

Daniel quickly redirected the senator's attention. "Senator, you remember Bob Solomon. Bob, come and say hi to Senator Wallace."

A man disengaged himself from a nearby conversation group and shook the senator's hand.

"Bob was a big supporter of the Nicholson campaign," said Daniel.

The senator's grin broadened.

Daniel eased Amanda away from the conversation.

"What I want to know," she said, "is, if the economic clout is no longer in the hands of the Fortune 500, who the hell does he think has it?"

"Let's move on," said Daniel.

"Let's move upstairs," said Amanda.

He glanced down at her. "Upstairs?"

Amanda stopped and faced him. She had planned to have a drink, maybe two or three before this moment, but she didn't think she could last much longer.

"I have a confession."

His brows went up. "Do tell."

"I rented a room."

"You *what?*"

"I—"

"Wait. Damn." He latched on to her arm and spun her around. "Keep walking. Don't look back."

"Is it your parents?"

"No, it's not my parents. Jeez, Amanda. They like you already."

"No they don't."

He scooted her around a corner where they were hidden from the main ballroom. Rich burgundy curtains accented paned glass doors that led to a balcony overlooking Fifth Avenue. It had started to rain, so nobody was outside. Wet droplets blurred the city lights and darkened the secluded corner.

"Who did we escape from?" she asked.

"Sharon."

Amanda blinked at him. They were hiding from his ex-wife? Why did he have to hide her from Sharon?

"She's been…" He tightened his jaw. "Difficult."

Amanda's stomach lurched. Maybe she'd got this all wrong. Maybe her imagination and Karen's enthusiasm had led her down a completely wrong path.

She took a couple of steps back. "Hey, if you've still got a thing for—"

Daniel reached out and grasped her arms, halting her retreat. "I do *not* have a thing for Sharon." He loosened his grip and closed the space between them. "It's just that she's loud and unpredictable. I didn't want her to insult you."

"Insult me?"

He shifted closer still, and his voice went gravelly. "Forget Sharon. Let's get back to the part where you rented a room."

Amanda's heart flip-flopped.

"You rented a room?" he prompted, his blue eyes smoldering with obvious desire.

She drew in a bracing breath. This was going to be even harder than she'd imagined.

His voice dropped to a whisper. "I rented a room here once."

"Yeah?" she managed.

His eyes twinkled like a moonlit ocean. "It was prom night. And I got very, *very* lucky."

Amanda ducked her head and focused on his chest.

"Hey." He tipped her chin up with his finger. "Is it possible that you're propositioning me?"

She slowly nodded. "It's possible."

A broad grin grew on his face. "All right."

His palm slid around to cup her cheek, and he dipped his head to kiss her.

She stretched to meet him, her muscles tense, her entire body humming with pent-up need.

His lips touched hers, and her limbs all but melted. He opened wide without preamble, stroking her tender mouth with the tip of his tongue. Her pulse pounded and their bodies fused with delicious heat.

Her hands twined around his neck, clinging to him, while he braced a forearm over the small of her back, holding her solid.

Their kiss deepened and lengthened. The orchestra music faded to the background and the pounding of the raindrops drummed in her ears.

"Mandy," he whispered, stroking her face with the pad of his thumb as he stared into her eyes for a long moment.

He returned to her lips. He grasped her buttocks, emphasizing his arousal. Amanda felt her bones turn to liquid.

"Daniel," she whimpered.

"Uh-hmm." A male voice sounded from behind her.

Amanda wrenched back, whipping her head around to see the senator, Sharon and two other people staring in shocked silence.

Nine

Daniel could think of a dozen directions this could go in. All of them bad. He'd wanted to thumb his nose at Sharon's orders, but this wasn't anywhere near what he'd had in mind.

Sharon's eyes glittered like granite; her mouth was drawn into a thin line of anger.

Senator Wallace looked faintly amused. He offered a quick salute with his single malt before turning to leave.

The Wilkinsons had the good grace to simply fade back into the party.

Sharon, on the other hand, advanced. "Have you lost your mind?"

"Do we really need to do this?" asked Daniel, keeping an arm around Amanda. The seven-figure settlement should have wedged Sharon out of his life for good.

"Yes, we need to do this. What did I ask you? What did I *tell* you?"

Amanda started to pull away. "I think I'll just—"

"Don't you go anywhere," Daniel demanded, tightening his hold on her waist.

Her eyes widened, and he moderated his voice. "Please wait." He turned to Sharon. "Go back to the party."

"Not a hope in hell. I'll be the laughingstock."

"Only if you act like it."

"You don't think this story has already circulated the room a dozen times?"

"It's been three minutes."

She leaned forward and poked him in the chest with her index finger. "You're the one who screwed up here, Daniel. And you're the one who's going to fix it."

"Don't be melodramatic."

"You are going to dance with me."

"What?"

"I mean it, Daniel. You get your butt out on that dance floor and let everybody see us laughing and talking together. That'll tamp down the gossip."

"Not in a million—"

"You owe me."

"I do not owe you anything."

Amanda shifted away again, this time breaking Daniel's grip.

He didn't blame her. Who wanted to watch a fight between a divorced couple? It probably brought back terrible memories for her.

He realized in an instant that if he wanted to get anywhere in his relationship with Amanda, he had to neutralize Sharon. And, right now, neutralizing Sharon meant dancing with her.

"Fine," he spat out reluctantly. He turned to Amanda. "This will only take a minute. Meet me by the statue?"

"Sure," she agreed with a shrug and an enigmatic expression.

Sharon grasped his arm, and he followed her onto the dance floor.

But halfway through the fake dance, Daniel spotted Amanda. She was leaving.

He swore under his breath and abandoned Sharon, practically sprinting for the exit.

"Amanda." Halfway across the foyer, he caught her by the arm. "What are you doing?"

She turned a glare on him. "You'd better get back to the party, Daniel. You wouldn't want people to gossip."

"I don't care if people gossip." He'd just left Sharon fuming in the middle of the dance floor. The gossip was well under way.

"Yes, you do," said Amanda.

"I was just trying to get rid of her."

"By dancing with her?"

"You saw what happened."

"Yeah. I saw exactly what happened."

"So you know—"

"Did you or did you not just blow me off for the sake of appearances?"

"It wasn't like that." He didn't care what people thought. He'd just wanted to get Sharon out of their hair.

"It was *exactly* like that. Not that I ever had any doubts." She shook her head and started walking again.

"Amanda." He matched his pace to hers.

"This was a mistake, Daniel."

"What was a mistake?"

"You, me, us. Thinking we could have the best of both worlds."

He blinked at her. "What best of both worlds?"

"Never mind."

"No. Not never mind. You have a room. *We* have a room."

She rolled her eyes and scoffed. "Right. We're going to sneak upstairs together. What if the senator sees you? What if your *parents* see you?"

"I don't care."

"Yes, you do."

He took her arm and tried to turn her around. "Let's go. You and me. Upstairs. Right now."

She shook him off. "Well, isn't that just the most romantic invitation I've ever had."

Daniel clenched his jaw.

A doorman pulled the glass door open.

"Good night, Daniel," said Amanda, shaking off his arm.

Short of throwing her bodily over his shoulder, Daniel had no choice but to watch her walk away.

"Good morning." Cullen strolled jauntily into Daniel's office. "I hear you had a date with Mom on the weekend."

"Where'd you hear that?" Daniel growled. He'd been trying to get Amanda on the phone for the past thirty-six hours.

"Aunt Karen told Scarlet, and Scarlet told Misty."

"Word travels fast in this family."

Cullen straddled a guest chair. "How'd it go?"

Daniel glared. He was pissed at Sharon and a little bit pissed at Amanda.

He'd done the right thing for them. He'd done the right thing for *her*. Sharon was poison, and they didn't need her out gunning for them.

"What?" asked Cullen, studying Daniel's expression. "I don't need intimate details or anything. 'Course if Mom's giving them to Karen, I'm going to hear eventually, anyway."

"Where are the weekly sales figures?"

Cullen drew back. "You want to talk *business?*"

"We're in the office, aren't we?"

"But—"

"And whatever happened with the Guy Lundin situation?" The time theft issue had been nagging in the back of Daniel's mind for a week. Not that he wanted to adopt Amanda's style of business management—far from it. He just wanted to understand what had happened, and how they could avoid it in the future.

"The time theft thing?" Cullen squinted. "Are you saying that me asking about Mom on company time is the same thing as a bogus sick claim?"

"Depends on how long you talk about her. Did we fire him?"

"I'm meeting with personnel this afternoon."

"What's your gut telling you?"

Cullen looked confused. "My gut?"

"Yeah. Your gut."

Cullen paused. "You already have all the verifiable facts."

He might have all the verifiable facts, but Daniel kept hearing Amanda's voice inside his head asking him how well he knew his employees. "What about the nonverifiable ones?"

"They're not relevant."

"Are there any?"

"Guy Lundin claims he was taking his mother to the cancer clinic."

"Did we check on that?"

Cullen sat down in one of the guest chairs. "There was no reason to check."

"Why not?"

"There's no provision for taking family members to medical appointments."

"So what do people do?" Daniel had taken Amanda out for a drink on company time. He'd ordered her flowers on company time. If she was sick, you can bet your ass he'd take her to the doctor on company time.

"About what?" asked Cullen.

"Family medical appointments. Emergencies. Crises."

Cullen held up his hands. "I don't know."

"Well, maybe we should think about it. Do you think Guy's mother is really sick?"

"He's not habitual about sick leave. He only took one day last year. Two the year before."

"Let's drop it," said Daniel, picking up his pen and flipping to a letter waiting for his signature.

"But my meeting—"

"Cancel the Personnel meeting. Give the guy a break."

"What about the other employees?"

"What about them?"

"What happens next time somebody has a sick family member?"

"Good question."

"Thank you."

Daniel pushed the intercom. "Nancy?"

"Yes?"

"Do we have a copy of the employee manual?"

"Yes, we do. Shall I bring it in?"

"Not yet."

"Okay."

Cullen leaned forward in his chair. "What are you doing?"

"Answering your question." Daniel waved him away. "Don't worry about it."

"You want to go over the sales report now?"

Daniel stood up and flexed his shoulders. "Nah. You take care of it. Let me know if there's anything I need to worry about."

Cullen stood with him. "You sure?"

"You're a good sales manager. I ever mention that?"

"Dad?"

Daniel rounded the desk and clapped his son on the shoulder. "No. You're a great sales manager."

"You okay?"

"Not really." He urged Cullen toward the door. "But I'm working on it."

Cullen looked at him strangely, but allowed himself to be ushered into the reception area.

As Cullen left, Daniel stopped beside Nancy's desk. "Can you do a little research for me?"

She picked up a pad and pen. "Of course."

"Find some comparable-size companies and see if anybody has family leave."

"Family leave?"

"For sick kids and stuff."

Nancy gazed at him.

"Time off. When your kids are sick, or your parents have medical appointments."

"Is this about Guy Lundin?"

Daniel smiled. "I definitely hired you for your brain."

"I'll get right on it," she said.

Daniel turned. Then he turned back. "How's your family?"

She squinted at him, hesitating for a second. "They're fine."

"Your kids are…"

"Sarah's nine and Adam's seven."

"Right. They like school?"

Nancy blinked. "Yes."

Daniel nodded. "That's good." He tapped his knuckles on her desk before turning to walk back into his office.

Sarah and Adam. He'd have to make a note of that.

He eased down into his chair again and picked up his phone. He had Amanda's office number memorized now, so he dialed it directly.

"Amanda Elliott's office," Julie answered.

"Hi, Julie. It's Daniel."

"I'm not supposed to put you through."

"Yeah, I figured that."

"You wanna bribe me?"

Daniel chuckled, liking Julie better and better all the time. "What'll it take?"

"Some more of those gold foil chocolates Amanda brought in."

"They'll be on your desk in an hour."

"Amanda can speak with you right away." The line clicked and went silent.

"Amanda Elliott."

"It's me."

Silence.

"I took your advice today." He waited.

"What advice?"

Bingo. He'd have put money on that line working. "I've ordered a review of family leave provisions for the employee manual."

"Ordered?"

"Okay. I asked my secretary to look into it. Her kids' names are Sarah and Adam, by the way."

"You had to find that out, didn't you?"

"I think the important point here is that I *did* find that out."

"Okay. I'll give you credit for that." There was a smile in her voice.

He jumped at the opening. "Go out with me again, Amanda."

"Daniel—"

"Anywhere you want. Anything you want. You name it."

"This is not going to work."

Panic surged in the pit of his stomach. "You can't know that. We don't even know what we're doing, where we're going. If you don't know what *this* is, how can you know that it won't work?"

"You ever thought of becoming a litigator?"

"What's your gut telling you, Amanda?"

"My gut?"

"Your instincts. You're the one who's big on instinct and spontaneity. Forget logic—"

"Forget logic?"

He slowed himself down. "Go with emotion on this one, Amanda. If I can take your advice, surely you can take it, too."

Her voice went soft. "That's not fair, Daniel."

He matched his tone to hers. "Who said anything about fair?"

She sighed. "Anywhere I want?"

"Yeah."

"A picnic. At the beach."

"Sunday at five."

She hesitated for another couple of heartbeats. "All right."

"I'll pick you up."

"No limo."

"I promise."

To be fair, Amanda had only specified that he couldn't use a limo. Too bad she hadn't thought to ban helicopters.

The chopper set them down on the helipad of the Carmichael estate on Nantucket. The Carmichaels were in London, but they'd given Daniel permission to use their private beach. And apparently they'd offered their staff, as well, or else Daniel had hired staff specifically for the occasion.

It *was* on the beach. And there *was* food. But that was where the resemblance to a picnic ended.

A round table had been set up on a flat stretch of sand between the lapping waves and the rocky cliffs. A white tablecloth flapped in the light breeze, held down by flowers, hurricane lamps, crystal and fine china. A maître d' stood at attention, and he appeared to be wearing a Secret Service headset.

Daniel pulled out one of the padded chairs and gestured for her to sit down. "I asked them to time the entrée for sunset."

"*This* is a picnic?" As soon as her butt hit the cushion, the maître d' sprang into action.

He muttered something into his microphone then laid her napkin across her lap.

"We're starting with margaritas," Daniel said, sitting down across from her.

"Margaritas?" asked Amanda.

"I hope you like them. If not, I can arrange—"

"I like them just fine. But, Daniel…"

"Yes?"

"This isn't a picnic."

He glanced around. "What do you mean?"

"A picnic is fried chicken and chocolate cake on a blanket, battling ants—"

"I think we can skip the ants."

"—maybe cheap wine in paper cups."

"Now you're just being ornery. People drink margaritas on beaches all over the world."

"At resorts. They don't bring a blender to a picnic. Where would you plug it in?"

"Who brought a blender?"

"That's how you get margaritas."

"The bartender is making them in the house. Now relax."

At that moment, the bartender appeared with two frosty lime margaritas in hand. At least Amanda thought it was the bartender. Perhaps Daniel had also hired a cocktail waiter.

Daniel thanked the man, who then withdrew back up the wooden stairs to the house.

Amanda took a sip of her margarita. It was delicious. It just wasn't rustic.

"We're starting with a shrimp Creole appetizer," said Daniel.

"Stop trying to impress me." She hadn't come here to see Daniel's money at work. She'd come here to see Daniel.

He sat back. "This is a date. Why wouldn't I try to impress you?"

Maybe it was time to tell him she was a sure thing. She smiled to herself. Before this night was over, she was going to fight her way through to the real Daniel, then she was making love to him.

"What?" he asked, watching her smile.

She tucked her hair behind her ears. "I was wondering about the employee manual."

"Nancy did a terrific job researching. We're putting forward a proposal to Dad."

"You're going to offer family leave?"

"We're going to propose it."

Amanda took a sip of the tart margarita. "What made you change your mind?"

"About looking at my employees as people?"

She nodded.

"You did, of course."

She felt a warm glow. "Thank you."

"No. Thank *you*. You push and prod and poke and probe—"

"You make me sound so appealing."

He grinned. "You are rather relentless."

"So are you."

"Hey, I gave up."

She stilled. He made an interesting point. Daniel had sincerely tried to understand her perspective, whereas she hadn't budged a single inch.

The rhythm of the waves increased and a group of gulls called on the air currents high above.

Amanda flicked her hair out of her eyes.

"What's wrong?" he asked.

She shook her head and revived her smile. "Nothing. Tell me about the CEO competition."

"What about it?"

"Are you going to win?"

Daniel shrugged. "We're coming up fast on Web site subscriptions."

"There are four months left."

"But *Charisma* always has a strong December."

Amanda nodded, toying with the stem on her frosted glass. "Will you be disappointed if you lose?"

He looked her straight in the eye. "Of course. I play to win."

"I know. But ego aside—"

"I don't have an ego."

Amanda laughed. "Oh, Daniel."

He looked genuinely confused. "What?"

"You mean to tell me having the job is more important than winning the game?"

"I don't know what you're talking about. It's the same thing."

She shook her head, flicking her hair again as the breeze freshened. "It's two completely different things."

"How?"

Another uniformed waiter appeared with their appetizer. After he left, Daniel asked his question again. "How?"

Amanda took a deep breath, trying to figure out how to say what she wanted to say. "Take off your jacket."

"What?"

"You heard me."

When he didn't move, she stood up and walked around to his chair. As she reached for his lapels, storm clouds rumbled on the distant horizon.

He pulled back. "What are you doing?"

She grasped his jacket and tugged it over his shoulders. "I'm peeling away the layers."

"The layers?"

"To get to the real you."

"I think that's metaphorical. And I *am* the real me."

She tugged on his sleeve. "How do you know?"

He finally gave up and shrugged out of his jacket. "Because I've been the real me my entire life."

Amanda went to work on his tie. "What does the real you want?"

He looked straight into her eyes. "You."

Okay. That was a good answer. "I meant professionally."

"I want to be CEO. Why is it so inconceivable to you that

I want the top job in a company where I've worked my whole life?"

She released the knot in his tie and pulled it from around his neck. "Because I think people, your family, have been putting things in front of you for forty years and then telling you you're supposed to want them."

"Like what?"

She dropped the tie on the table. "For starters? Me."

He looked to his right and then to his left. "I don't see my family urging me on here."

"I meant after high school."

He pulled her into his lap. "Hey, that was just you and me on prom night. Nobody *told* me to want you."

"They told you to marry me."

"You were pregnant."

"They told you to come back to the family firm."

"We needed the money."

"They told you to stay on this continent."

Daniel snapped his jaw shut. "I stayed for you."

She shook her head. "You stayed because they told you to stay. Whose idea was it for you to marry Sharon?"

"Mine." But he flinched, then went quiet.

"Whose idea was it for you to try for the CEO position?"

Daniel stared at her.

"What do *you* want, Daniel?"

Thunder boomed closer this time, and lightning flashed in the darkening sky as the first fat drops of rain hit the sand.

Daniel turned to the maître d'. "Have them bring out the canopy, Curtis."

Amanda jumped up from Daniel's lap. "No!"

"What?"

"No canopy."

"Why not?"

"Layers, Daniel."

He peered at her. "Are you, like, clinically insane?"

She leaned closer. "Can you send that man away?"

"Will I be safe alone with you?"

"Maybe."

He hesitated, and another thunderclap echoed against the cliffs. "You can go inside, Curtis. We'll be fine."

Curtis nodded and headed for the staircase.

"So, we're going to stay out here and get wet?" Daniel asked.

"Yeah. Life's messy. Get used to it."

"Can I put my jacket back on?"

"No."

"You want it?"

The rain began in earnest, and Amanda spread her arms wide. "No."

"Dinner's ruined," he pointed out.

"We'll order pizza later."

"What do we do now?"

"Now?" She climbed back into his lap, wrapping her arms around his dampening shirt and slicking back his wet hair.

This was Daniel. This was real. This was what she'd been waiting for.

"Now," she said, "we make love."

Ten

Daniel stared at Amanda's wet hair, her clingy blouse and her loose chinos.

He'd pictured this moment, pictured it a million times. But there was always a bed, satin sheets, champagne. "Here?"

"Yeah." She laughed, kicking out her legs. "Right here."

"You'll get cold."

"I don't care."

He glanced at the yachts moored in the bay. "Somebody might see us."

"They'd need a telephoto lens."

"Yeah." As if that had ever been a deterrent.

"Afraid you'll end up on the cover of your own magazine?"

"Don't be ridiculous, Amanda."

"Kiss me, Daniel."

He gazed at her moist mouth. It was tempting. Boy, was it tempting. "You'll get sand stuck to your butt."

"My butt will survive."

He wanted this to be memorable. He wanted this to be perfect. He wanted this to be a moment she'd cherish. "Can we at least go inside?"

She leaned forward and placed a quick kiss on his mouth. "Not a chance."

Her lips were cool and damp and sexy as hell.

"Amanda," he groaned in protest.

"Here and now, wet and wild, cold and sandy, risking yachting voyeurs." She kissed him again, longer this time, deeper, their lips warming to each other.

"I don't remember you being like this," he mumbled before initiating the next kiss.

"You weren't paying close enough attention." She plucked at the buttons of his shirt.

Losing track of the argument, he returned the favor, separating the fabric of her blouse and sliding his hand beneath it. "Oh, yes, I was," he breathed, inhaling deeply. "I remember every square inch of your skin."

"Every single one?"

"Yeah."

"You want to see them again?"

He spared one more worried glance at the boats bobbing just offshore. It was getting pretty dark. If he spread his coat behind the skirt of the tablecloth, her modesty would be well protected.

Curtis wouldn't let any of the staff come back down unless Daniel called for them.

"Yes," he answered, making the only possible decision. "Oh, yes."

Amanda pulled back, shifting so that she straddled his lap. Then she gave him a saucy, mischievous grin and slowly peeled away the wet fabric of her blouse, baring her breasts.

Lightning flashed, and her alabaster skin glowed slick in the white light.

His world stilled. Unable to stop himself, he leaned forward and kissed one breast, then the other, tasting her delicate skin, testing the texture with his tongue, drawing out the moment, second after exquisite second. Her skin was as sweet as he remembered. He used to crave her taste, revel in her scent, count the minutes until he could hold her and become one with her.

The raindrops clattered, and the waves roared onto the shore. The thunder rumbled the very earth beneath them, but he blanked out everything but the gorgeous woman in his arms. Her skin was slick and wet, and impossibly smooth. Her murmurs of encouragement stoked his desire.

He couldn't stop holding her, but he *had* to make love to her. He finally stood, lifting her with him and holding her close. Her legs wrapped around his waist, and she burrowed her face in his neck, lips suckling, tongue laving his sensitive skin.

He lowered her feet to the sand, kissing her deeply as he flicked his coat out on the wet beach.

She stepped back, peeling away the rest of her wet clothes, and the lightning flashes gave him tantalizing glimpses of her naked body—her rounded breasts, the tight pink nipples, her smooth stomach and the dark triangle that led between her legs.

Every muscle in his body grew taut, and he reached out a trembling hand to cup her hip.

It was like the Boca Royce pool, only better than the pool. Her curves were wet and smooth and ripe, but this time he could touch her. He could hold her. He could make the world melt away between them.

"You're gorgeous," he whispered, slowly drawing her toward him. His arms wrapped around her naked body, and raw lust overtook his system. There was something incredibly erotic about a naked woman on a dark, windswept beach. For a split second he wondered why they'd never done this before.

Then, impatient, he laid her back on the blanket of his coat, shucking his clothes, following her down, putting them out of the wind, behind the protection of the tablecloth.

She smiled at his nakedness, her gaze caressing his entire body. Then she reached for him, twining her fingers in his damp hair, cupping his face and urging him down for a long, searing kiss.

The raindrops practically sizzled against his heated skin. She was the sexiest, most amazing woman alive, and it was all he could do to keep from taking her in the next five seconds.

He gulped in mouthfuls of salt air and steeled himself against the onslaught of desire.

"I've missed you," she whispered.

A steel band tightened around his chest, and he thought it might explode. He cupped her face, kissing her sweet lips, absorbing her taste, reveling in her feel. "Oh, Amanda, this is so…"

"Real?"

He nodded.

Her hair was tangled with wet sand, her makeup was smeared in a rainbow, and droplets of water trickled over her cheeks. But he'd never seen a more beautiful woman. Sensation washed over him with the beat of the waves. "I remember."

"Me, too. I remember you were wonderful."

"I remember you were beautiful."

Her hands tightened on his upper arms. "I want you. Right now."

He shook his head. "Not yet." There was nothing he wanted more. And nothing would stop him, nothing could possibly come between them.

But he had to make this last. He had to imprint her on his brain all over again. There'd be many long, lonely nights ahead, and he wanted hot memories to see him through.

He was selfish, he knew. But he couldn't help himself.

He cupped her breast, feeling the press of her taut nipple against his palm.

She moaned.

"You like?" he asked.

She nodded her head.

He brushed a thumb across the crest, and her fingertips convulsed against him.

Her response was fuel to his fire, and he let his hands and lips roam free, changing her breathing to gasps and pants, reveling in his ability to please her.

He trailed his fingers up her thigh, finding the core of her heat, groaning aloud as he pressed into her softness. She welcomed him with a flex of her hips, and her mocha eyes went wide.

"Oh, Daniel."

"I know." He kissed her deeply. "I know. Just go with it."

She responded, running her fingers over his chest, finding his flat nipples, his navel, his abdomen, and sending shock waves straight through his body.

Then her cool, small hands roamed farther, grasping him, stroking him, urging him.

He shifted above her.

"Now," she asked again, tightening her grip.

His only response was a guttural groan. He pushed her thighs apart, kissing her lips, her cheeks, her eyes as he pressed inside her inch by careful inch.

She gasped his name.

He almost shouted "I love you." But that was a different time, a different place.

"Amanda," he gasped instead, surging into a rhythm as her hips rocked forward and her legs locked around his waist.

He cupped her breast, and she gripped his shoulders, her nails digging into his skin. Her head dropped back and she scrunched her eyes shut.

The thunder rumbled and the waves crashed their furor.

There could have been an armada of paparazzi moored in the bay and he couldn't have cared less. She was his. After all these years, she was his once again.

Her teeth clamped down on her bottom lip, and her breathing became ragged. He could feel her body arching against him, straining, struggling.

He waited, waited, waited.

"Daniel!" she cried, and he let himself go.

The lightning melted the sky and the earth shook with the force of his release.

When it was over, they lay gasping in each other's arms. Daniel supported himself on his elbows, using his body heat to keep her warm.

He kissed her forehead and lingered there, because he simply couldn't resist. He knew they should get dressed and go up to the house to dry off, but he didn't have it in him to let her out of his arms.

She smiled, her eyes still closed. "I just love spontaneity."

His heart contracted on the word *love*. But that wasn't what she meant. He brushed a lock of gritty hair from her check. "What makes you think I didn't plan this?"

Her eyes popped open. "You did not."

"Sure, I did."

"Daniel, this is not a plan you would make."

He nodded. "What's more, you planned it, too."

"Dream on."

"Counselor, are you trying to tell me you didn't plan to make love with me tonight?"

"I didn't know when, and I didn't know how."

He shifted his weight and leaned on one elbow. "That's still a plan."

She wiggled as cool air blew between their bodies and the slowing rain trickled over their hot skin. "No, that's an idea."

"Semantics."

"Philosophy."

He chuckled. "Admit it, your philosophy's not that much different than mine."

She shifted on his wrinkled coat, propping on her elbow, a gleam in her eye. "You think? Okay. Let's talk philosophy. Tell me again why you want to be CEO?"

He groped for his dress shirt, shook it out with one hand and draped it over her. "The corner office."

"You already have a corner office."

"Yeah, but this one's on the twenty-third floor."

"Weak, Daniel. Very weak."

"You're making more of this than actually exists."

She shook her head. "No, I'm not. Your father told you to fight for the CEO job."

"And I'm fighting because *I* want it. Not because somebody told me to want it." But even as he made the argument, he felt a crack in it.

Had he ever thought about becoming CEO before his father had issued the challenge? He'd jumped right in, along with his three siblings, but he'd never stopped to analyze the decision.

Amanda continued to challenge him. "Tell me the last thing you aspired to that wasn't suggested by someone else."

He focused on her earnest face. "Changing the employee manual."

Amanda made a negative buzzer sound. "That was my idea."

"Not specifically."

"But generally. You remember prom night?"

He tucked his shirt closer around her. "In detail."

"You remember your adventure magazine plan?"

"Of course."

She traced a fingertip along the ridge of his bicep, and suddenly his body was awash in heat. "That was you, Daniel. That was *all* you."

He nodded, thinking she was proving his point rather than her own.

"What happened to that?" she asked.

What a crazy question. "Bryan happened to it. *You* happened to it."

"You ever think about where you'd be if you'd done it anyway?"

Daniel shifted his gaze past the top of her head to the black cliffs and the faint lights of the mansion. "No," he lied.

"Never?"

He shrugged. "What's the point?"

She curled into a sitting position, his shirt falling to her lap. "There's every point. I wonder all the time what would have happened if I'd told Patrick to take a flying leap."

"A flying leap to where?"

She flipped her damp hair back. "You know. Told him to bugger off. Gone to court over Bryan, and sent you off to Africa or the Middle East."

A chill formed deep inside Daniel. Gone to court?

"Maybe he was bluffing." She got a faraway look, and Daniel pushed into a sitting position.

A sense of dread crept along his veins. "Bluffing how?"

Amanda bit her lower lip, a bleak vulnerability coming into her eyes. "You think a judge would have taken a baby away from its mother? Even back then?"

Daniel's throat went dry. He shook his head, sure he couldn't be hearing what he thought he was hearing. "Patrick threatened to take Bryan away from you?" he rasped.

"Yeah…" Her brown eyes darkened. She squinted at Daniel. "You didn't—"

He shot to his feet and paced down the sand before pivoting on his heel and raking a hand through his wet hair. "My father threatened to take Bryan away from you?"

She stood up. "It was a long time ago. I thought you…"

His hands tightened into fists as every muscle in his body clenched. "You thought I knew?"

She nodded. Then she shook her head. "I'm sorry. I shouldn't have brought it up. You're right, there's no point in discussing what-ifs."

Daniel forced himself to take three deep breaths. It wasn't Amanda's fault, nothing was Amanda's fault. She'd been forced to marry him.

This answered *so* many questions. All those years, she'd let herself be kept hostage for the sake of her children. It was a wonder she'd lasted as long as she did.

In an instant, Daniel knew Amanda was right. Patrick was more insidious than he had ever imagined. What else had he done? How much manipulation went on in the Elliott family?

Did Daniel want to become CEO?

He had nothing against being CEO. But was being CEO where he wanted to put all his effort, all his energy, all his time?

Not a question he could answer at the moment, and not one he had any intention of pondering while Amanda was shivering on a beach.

He drew a cleansing breath and moved toward her. "I'm the one who's sorry," he said, gently drawing her into his embrace. "My father should *not* have done that. I had no idea you'd been blackmailed."

She shivered in his arms. "It was a long time ago."

He nodded against the top of her head, kissing her sand-gritty hair. "It was a long time ago."

She tipped her chin to look up at him. "Can we do spontaneity again sometime?"

He stroked a hand over her hair. "Anytime, anyplace."

Her lips curved into a brilliant smile.

Daniel gritted his teeth as he crossed the twenty-third floor to his father's office at eight o'clock on Monday. He would have confronted him last night, but he didn't want to do this in front of his mother.

"Hello, Daniel," Patrick's secretary greeted.

"I need to see him," said Daniel. "Now."

"I'm afraid that's not possible."

"Take a good look at my expression. Now."

Mrs. Bitton pulled her glasses down the bridge of her nose. "Take a good look at my expression."

Normally, Mrs. Bitton intimidated the hell out of Daniel, but not today.

"Pull him out," said Daniel.

An unexpected grin tugged at the corner of her mouth. "Bad idea."

"I really don't give a damn what he's doing."

"He's at thirty-thousand feet over Texas."

Daniel paused. "When does he get in?"

"He'll be here at two. But he's meeting with the art director."

"Rebook."

"Daniel—"

"Look into my eyes, Mrs. Bitton."

She paused. "I can put it off until two-thirty."

Daniel gave her a sharp nod. "Good enough."

Amanda knew it was barely twelve hours since they'd left the beach. But Daniel *had* said anytime, anyplace. Plus, now that she'd wedged the door open a crack, she was determined to drag him out of his regimented little world.

She paused at Nancy's desk, holding up the bag of Buster Burgers. "Is he free?"

Nancy's eyes lit up and her lips curved into an amazed smile. She pressed her intercom button. "Mrs. Elliott to see you."

There was a silent pause. "Fine," said Daniel, his voice abrupt.

Amanda hesitated, but Nancy waved her toward the door. "Don't worry about it. He's having a tense morning. You'll cheer him up."

Amanda headed across the outer office. She sure hoped she would. Slipping through the door, she flipped the lock behind her.

Daniel glanced up from his desk.

His eyes widened, and he drew back. "Amanda?"

"Who were you expecting?"

He shook his head and stood up. "Nobody. Nothing." He rounded the wide, thankfully empty desk. "I'm glad you're here."

"Good. I brought lunch."

He looked down at the bag, and his eyebrows shot up. "Buster Burgers?"

"Ever tried one?"

"Can't say that I have."

She dropped the bag on his desk. "They're to die for."

His glance strayed past her. "You locked the door?"

She sidled up to him. "I locked the door." She ran her fingertips down his silver silk tie. "You did say anytime, anyplace."

His jaw dropped, and his hands closed over hers, stilling them. "Amanda."

She grinned. "This is anytime. This is anyplace. And I'm here for spontaneity."

"Yeah, right."

She shook her head and freed her hands, going to work on the knot of his tie.

"Are you nuts?"

"No."

"What if somebody—"

"Have a little faith in Nancy."

"But—"

She ran her tongue around the rim of her lips and gazed

deeply into his blue eyes. "I've been wanting to do you on the desktop since the first time you walked into my office."

His jaw worked, but no sound came out.

She pulled off his tie and started on his buttons.

"You want burgers first?" she asked, leaning forward to give him a hot, wet kiss on the chest. "Or you want me?"

He made a sound that was half groan, half curse and his arms wrapped tightly around her waist. He kissed her hair, murmuring her name over and over.

"We can be quick," she assured him, kicking off her shoes. "I'm alfresco under this skirt."

He dipped his head to kiss her mouth.

She opened wide, and liquid desire poured through her system. She pushed his shirt out of the way, reveling in the feel of his hot skin against her fingertips.

He held her close, while one hand snaked its way up her thigh.

He groaned when he reached her bare buttocks. Then he turned her and lifted her onto the desk, pushing her skirt out of the way without breaking their kiss.

He slipped his hands over her thighs, sensitizing her skin. Then he reached around to caress her bottom.

"What you do to me," he murmured as he massaged and kneaded, making her squirm against the smooth wood.

"What you do back," she breathed, burying her face in his neck, inhaling his scent.

"But I'm a little busy right now." His fingertips danced their way between her legs, tickling, teasing, tantalizing. "And I'm not sure this is the time or place—"

"Don't mess with me." She scrunched forward, urging his explorations to go further.

"Like you're not messing with me?"

"It's for your own good," she gasped, reaching down to press his hand into her.

He disentangled himself, but then dropped to his knees. "My own good?" He feathered light kisses along her inner thigh.

She sank back on her elbows. "Okay, this part's for my own good." Her muscles started to melt.

He chuckled against her, and moved higher, higher still, and then his voice vibrated on her tender flesh. "I think there's a company rule against this."

"Don't you dare stop."

"Maybe even two."

"Daniel."

He chuckled again, and then he kissed her, hard and deep, and a little bit of heaven zapped right down into *Snap*. She sucked in gulps of air, gripping the edge of the desk as he nearly drove her out of her mind.

She was soaring, flying, cresting…

Then she realized what he was doing, and she jerked away.

"What?" He looked up.

"Uh-uh." She sat up straight, latched on to his shoulders and pulled.

"You done?" he asked, slowly rising.

"Hardly." She went after the button on his slacks.

He grabbed her hand to stop her.

But she stroked him through the fabric and he groaned, grasping the edge of the desk with his free hand.

"You're mine, Daniel," she vowed.

"I can't…" He gritted his teeth, and the hand stopping her relaxed.

She popped the button. His zipper slid down easily, and her hand contacted searing hot flesh.

"Amanda—"

"Do me on the desktop, Daniel," she purred.

"You're out of your—"

She squeezed. "Now."

He swore.

She pressed forward, bringing him against her, guiding him inside her.

He swore again, but it sounded like a prayer, and he gathered her to him with a groan of surrender.

He slipped his hands right under her bottom, holding her in place while his body thrust, and his muscles bunched beneath his suit jacket, turning to tempered steel.

He whispered of how she looked, how she felt, how she tasted. She reveled in his words, his touch, his scent.

She lost track of time as the tension mounted and the room spun around. She frantically kissed his mouth, tangling with his tongue. His fingers dug into her as he groaned her name and jerked harder and harder against her.

Sensation radiated out like fireworks, and she slipped off the edge of the world, her body contracting over and over and over again.

When their heartbeats finally slowed, his hands were tangled in her hair. He gently kissed her temple, stroking his knuckles down her cheek.

"I'm beginning to love spontaneity," he breathed.

"You give a whole new meaning to the word," she admitted.

His chest puffed against her.

"Burger?" she asked.

Daniel laughed deep in his throat, and his arms contracted around her. "There's a bathroom through that door." He pointed. "If you want to freshen up."

She kissed his mouth. "Yeah."

He kissed her back. "Okay."

She kissed him again. "Hope you like cola."

He kissed her. "Sure."

She kissed him, and this time they lingered. "I guess we don't have time to do it again, huh?" she asked.

"Not and eat the burgers."

"You don't want to miss the burgers."

He stepped back, and she slid off the desk.

While she washed, and combed her hair, she could hear Daniel unpacking their lunch.

On the way back through the office, she scooped his tie from where it dangled over the back of a guest chair and looped it around her neck.

Daniel handed her a burger, taking the guest chair beside her.

"These aren't bad," he said after the first bite.

"Would I steer you wrong?" The waxed paper crackled as she unwrapped hers.

"Apparently not. Where did you get them?"

"Across the street. You know it's a national chain, right?"

"Really?"

She shook her head and laughed lightly. "There's a whole world out there you've never seen."

He stopped eating and gave her an intense stare. "You want to show it to me?"

Amanda felt a surge of guilt. He was coming around. He was willing to meet her halfway, to experience new things. And she still hadn't budged.

It wasn't Daniel's fault that Patrick was a Machiavellian genius. More than any of his siblings, Daniel had tried to exert his independence. And the fact that Bryan was the only Elliott who'd succeeded in breaking free was partly thanks to Daniel.

She swallowed, making a decision. "Only if you'll agree to show me your world."

He crumpled his wrapper and tossed it into the trash. "What do you want to see first? Paris? Rome? Sydney?"

"I was thinking more along the lines of The Met."

"You've already been to The Met."

"But you can get better tickets."

"*La Bohème,* followed by pizza?"

Amanda laughed and stood up, tossing her own wrapper in the trash. "I've got an appointment at one," she told him.

He moved in front of her, kissing her gently on the lips and reaching for his tie.

"Uh-uh." She shook her head and held the tie fast. "Souvenir."

"Fine," he agreed easily.

While she gathered her purse and took a last drink, he moved around the desk. He opened a drawer and extracted another tie.

Amanda dropped her paper cup in the bin and followed him around. She commandeered the second tie.

"Hey!"

"No tie."

He grabbed for it, but she backed away.

"What do you mean no tie?"

She looped the second one around her neck. "Price you pay for spontaneity."

"Nancy's going to know what happened."

Amanda shot him a grin. "Yeah, she will."

He took a step toward her. "Amanda—"

"Call me." She quickly scooted out the door.

Eleven

At precisely two o'clock, Daniel strode into his father's outer office. Making love with Amanda had taken the edge off his anger. Making love with Amanda had taken the edge off everything.

But then, making love with her had also reminded him all over again how cruelly his father had manipulated a frightened, pregnant teenager.

"Is he here?" Daniel asked Mrs. Bitton, barely breaking his stride.

"He's expecting you," she answered.

Daniel swung the door wide, then shut it firmly behind him.

His father didn't look up from the papers he was signing. "Do we have some kind of a problem?"

Daniel took a few steps into the office, struggling to keep a rein on his temper. "Yes, we have some kind of a problem."

Patrick glanced up. "And that would be…?"

"You blackmailed Amanda."

Patrick didn't flinch. "I haven't said more than three words to her in sixteen years."

Daniel took two more paces. "You threatened to take Bryan away from her." His voice rose, nearly shaking. "How could you do that? She was eighteen, pregnant, defenseless."

Patrick set down his pen and squared his shoulders. "I did what was best for the family."

Daniel smacked his palms on the desktop. "Best for you, yes. Best for the family, maybe. Best for Amanda? I don't think so."

"Amanda wasn't my responsibility."

"Amanda is my *wife!*" Daniel shouted.

"*Was* your wife."

Daniel clamped his jaw and sucked in a breath.

Patrick rose to his feet. "This is ancient history, Daniel. And I have a meeting."

"Don't you dare."

"Don't I *dare?*"

Daniel pointed a finger at his father's chest. Strangely, the man who had intimidated him all his life didn't look so intimidating now. "We're not finished with this conversation."

Patrick started around the desk. "We are *definitely* finished with this conversation, and you're damn lucky you still have a job."

Daniel stepped sideways, blocking his father's exit, folding his arms over his chest. "You are going to apologize to Amanda."

Patrick's eyes glittered and a muscle ticked in one jaw. "Amanda made her choice."

"You gave her *no* choice."

"She chose to sleep with you."

"You know nothing about what happened that night."

"Are you telling me she was unwilling?"

Something exploded in Daniel's brain. He doubled up his fists and leaned in. "Are you suggesting I raped her?"

"Did you?"

"No! Of course not!"

"Then she made her choice. There was a baby. An *Elliott* baby. I protected the family, and that's all I'm going to say on the matter." Patrick started to go around Daniel.

This time Daniel didn't stop him. His voice dropped to a growl. "You betrayed her, and you betrayed me."

Patrick's voice shook with anger. "I *protected* this family."

Daniel pivoted to glare at him. "You were wrong."

Patrick stared back for a long moment, then he walked out of the office.

Daniel hadn't had it in him to work the rest of the day. Going home held no appeal, and he was too upset to call Amanda.

He ended up at the family table at Une Nuit, Bryan's restaurant. Bryan wasn't there—just as well. Daniel was content to hunch in a dim corner and sip on his second single malt. He had a lot of thinking to do.

"Hey, bro." Michael slid into the chair in front of him.

"Hey," Daniel answered, checking to see if anyone was with Michael. He really didn't feel like company at the moment.

"Heard you reamed out the boss." Michael signaled to the manager for his usual drink.

Daniel nodded. He wondered how accurately the gossip had spread.

"Business matter?" asked Michael.

"Personal," said Daniel.

Michael accepted a martini from a waiter. "Amanda?"

Daniel squinted. "What did you hear?"

"That you ordered Mrs. Bitton to reschedule Dad's meeting—nice one, by the way—and that you went up one side of him and down the other." Michael took a swig of his drink. "And you're still standing."

"Still employed, too." Daniel was pretty amazed about that. Not that he'd cared at the time.

Michael snagged the olive from his martini and popped it into his mouth. "Only person I can think of that would make you go off like that is Amanda."

Daniel banged his heavy scotch glass on the table. "He threatened to take Bryan away from her if she didn't marry me."

Michael was silent for a moment. "I know."

"You *know?*"

Michael nodded. "He was afraid it would kill Mom to lose her grandchild."

"Why didn't you say something?"

"I was keeping my head low at the time. Remember, I was the guy who got you the suite."

"But later?"

"Later you two seemed happy. Then, when things fell apart, it hardly seemed like the kind of information that would help."

Daniel rocked back in his chair. "It was unconscionable."

Their brother Shane appeared and slid into the seat next to Daniel. "What was unconscionable?"

"Dad blackmailed Amanda into marrying Daniel," said Michael.

"When?" asked Shane.

Daniel turned to give his younger brother an amazed look. "In high school."

"Oh, that time."

"Was there another time?" Daniel asked.

"How'd he blackmail her?" asked Shane, ignoring his brother's comment.

Daniel chugged the last of his scotch, still seeing red at the thought of his father's actions. "He threatened to take Bryan away. He forced her to marry me in order to keep her baby."

Again, on cue, their sister Finola appeared and sat down next to Michael. "Could've been worse," she said.

Her three brothers' gazes swung her way.

Then they all went silent, remembering that Patrick had forced Finola to give up her own baby at fifteen.

Shane reached across the table and took his twin sister's hand. "Yeah, it could've."

"Aw, Fin," said Daniel, feeling like a jerk. At least he'd had the chance to raise Bryan.

Michael signaled for a round of drinks. "You ever wonder if this family needs therapy?"

Finola turned to look at her oldest brother, twin tears refusing to spill over her lashes. "What do you mean *wonder?* We're scrapping it out like a pack of dogs for our father's job."

Daniel dumped a sliver of ice into his mouth. "After this afternoon, it might be a three-way race."

Shane scoffed out a laugh. "What in the hell did you do?"

"I yelled at him," said Daniel.

"You *yelled* at Dad?" asked Finola, amazement clear in her voice.

"I ordered him to apologize to Amanda. I may have stopped him from leaving his office there for a minute, too."

"Bodily?" asked Michael.

"No blows were exchanged," said Daniel with a dark laugh.

Shane chuckled along with him.

"It may be a two-way race," said Michael.

Everyone turned their attention to him.

"With Karen's health I just don't have the energy for this. She needs me, and I am going to be there for her."

"Maybe I'll back out, too," said Shane.

"What are you talking about?" Michael asked Shane. "You have no reason to back out."

The waiter arrived and set drinks out all around.

"Don't be ridiculous," Finola said to Shane. "You love your job."

"I may love the job, but I hate being manipulated. He's hurt us all. At one time or another, he's screwed up everyone's life."

The other three nodded.

Daniel felt as though blinders had been peeled away from his eyes, and they could never be put back.

"When he made me take the job," said Daniel, "when Bryan was sick, and he told me it was the only way to clear the bills, it was the worst mistake I ever made." He pushed aside the memory of Bryan's heart defect, not wanting to relive the tense time before the surgery made his son whole.

Finola cocked her head. "But if you hadn't come back—"

"Amanda and I might still be married."

"Impoverished," said Michael.

"But married," said Shane, lifting his highball. "Chuck it, Daniel. Chuck it all and marry Amanda."

"Whoa," said Michael. "How'd we get there?"

Daniel laughed, but a small corner of his brain told him to take Shane seriously.

"You're bitter," Finola said to Shane.

Shane leaned forward and stage-whispered to his twin, "I'm cutting back the field. I'd rather have you in charge than Daniel."

Daniel elbowed Shane. "Hey. Why?"

"She likes me better than you do," Shane said to his brother.

"That's true enough," said Daniel.

Michael chomped down on his second olive. He waggled his eyebrows in Daniel's direction. "I don't think we can just let Finola walk away with it."

"Hell no," Daniel chuckled. "She's a girl."

Finola bristled. "Here we go again."

Amanda blinked, just to make sure it really was Sharon Elliott standing in her office doorway.

"Surprise," said Sharon, sauntering into the office in impossibly high heels, a black denim skirt and a black-and-white cropped sweater. Her hair was pulled back in a slick knot and her makeup was as bold as the outfit.

Julie made a face behind the woman's back and pulled the door shut.

Amanda closed her case file and came to her feet. "Can I help you with something?"

"Actually, it's me who's here to help you." Sharon pulled her deep red lips into a smile and sat down in one of the guest chairs, tucking her purse in the space beside her.

"Uh, thank you," said Amanda, dropping into her seat.

Sharon sat forward, jiggling her diamond teardrop earrings. The jeweled rings on her fingers flashed as she folded her hands. "I know what you're doing."

"You do?" Amanda was preparing closing arguments for the Spodek case, but she doubted that was what Sharon was talking about.

Sharon nodded. "And I can respect it."

"Thank you."

"But I think you might be fishing in the wrong pond."

"Oh?"

"Daniel is, let's say, challenging."

"Let's say." Amanda hoped being agreeable would get Sharon out of her office sooner.

Sharon reached for her purse, snapping open the clasp and retrieving a folded piece of paper. "I've taken the liberty of coming up with a list of potential men."

"For what?" asked Amanda.

"To date," said Sharon. She unfolded the paper, pasting on a just-between-us-girls smile. "They're all good-looking, intelligent, available and, most importantly, rich."

She held out the paper to Amanda.

Amanda gingerly took it. "You're showing me a list of your dates?"

Sharon's head tipped sideways, and her laughter tinkled though the office. "Not my dates," she said. "Yours."

Amanda dropped the paper. "*What?*"

Sharon shook her head. "Honey, Daniel is never going to fall for you again. Consider this a gift from one jilted wife to another."

Ah. It all made sense now. "I take it you want him back?"

"Me?" Sharon laughed again. It really was a lovely laugh. Probably lured men to their deaths all the time. "I'm not trying to get him back."

Sure, she wasn't. Sharon had decided to become dating.com out of the goodness of her heart.

Oh, wait. Sharon didn't have a heart. Which meant she was lying. She wanted Daniel back.

"Once you're on the outs with Patrick, you're on the outs," said Sharon.

Amanda supposed that was true enough.

"Though there was a time," Sharon continued, "that Patrick just couldn't get enough of me."

Amanda gave her head a little shake. "You *slept* with Patrick?"

"Of course not." Sharon dramatically fluttered her fingers against her chest. "He recruited me for Daniel. He knew exactly what he wanted in a daughter-in-law."

"And he got it," Amanda muttered, knowing Sharon was exactly what Patrick would have ordered.

"For a while." Sharon sighed. "Now, back to the list." She stood up and bent over to read upside down. "Giorgio is nice, not too tall, but very well-groomed. He has a penthouse overlooking the park, and—"

"Thank you," said Amanda, folding the list closed again. "But I'm not looking to date anyone."

Sharon straightened, her mouth drooping into a little-girl pout. "But—"

"I'm afraid I'm very busy." Amanda held out the list.

Sharon didn't take it. "You're dating Daniel."

"Not really." She was only sleeping with Daniel. That was

as far as the relationship was likely to go. Sharon was right about one thing, though: to get Daniel, first you needed Patrick.

The door opened, and Julie stuck her head in. "Amanda?"

Amanda could have kissed her receptionist.

"There's someone here to see you." Julie actually seemed flustered.

Amanda didn't care who it was, just so long as they got Sharon out of the office.

Amanda tucked the list into Sharon's hand. "Thanks for stopping by."

Julie opened the door wider.

Sharon glanced from one woman to the other. For a second, Amanda thought she was going to refuse to leave. But then she gritted her teeth, stood as tall as she was able and stalked to the door.

Suddenly, she halted in the doorway and swiveled her head to look back at Amanda. "It appears I underestimated you."

Before Amanda could decipher the cryptic message, Sharon was gone, and Patrick Elliott himself was entering the office.

She squeaked out a desperate signal to Julie, but Julie had already scooted out of the way.

"Amanda." Patrick's nod was terse as the door closed behind him.

"Mr. Elliott." Amanda nodded in return, her stomach clenching reflexively against her backbone. She couldn't remember the last time she'd been alone with him.

"Please, call me Patrick."

"All right." Now she was even more off balance.

He gestured to the guest chairs. "May I sit down?"

"Of course."

He waited, and she realized he expected her to sit first. She did, surreptitiously wiping her damp palms over her slacks.

He then took his own seat. "I'll get right to the point. My son tells me I owe you an apology."

Amanda opened her mouth. But then his words registered, and she promptly shut it again. She stared in silence at the man she'd feared for decades.

"I disagree with Daniel," Patrick continued. "I am not sorry."

Amanda let out her breath.

Okay, now he was sounding like himself. His hair might have gone completely white, and the line of his chin might have softened. But his ice-blue eyes were as shrewd as ever. The last thing in the world he'd do was arrive at her law office, hat in hand, begging for forgiveness.

"I'm not sorry I kept Bryan in the family," he continued. "And I'm not sorry I ensured Maeve had her grandchild. But I am sorry…" He paused, and his blue eyes thawed ever so slightly. "I am sorry that I didn't have your best interests at heart."

Amanda gave her head a little shake. Her ears must have been playing tricks on her. Had Patrick Elliott just apologized?

The corners of his mouth turned up. But it looked more like a grimace than a smile.

"It was a long time ago," said Amanda, realizing belatedly that she should have thanked him. Maybe. What on earth was the proper etiquette in these circumstances?

He nodded. "It was a long time ago. But Daniel's right. You were alone and frightened and I took advantage." He held up his palms. "Oh, I know I did the right thing. On balance, Bryan deserved to grow up an Elliott every bit as much as we deserved to know our grandchild. But…" His mouth pursed. "Let's just say I didn't have the same appreciation for collateral damage back then."

Amanda's spine stiffened ever so slightly. "Is that what you considered me? Collateral damage?"

Could a person actually live and breathe this many years without a soul?

"I considered your circumstance…unfortunate," he said.

"Yet you played God." Despite his apology, decades of anger surged through her bloodstream. She hadn't deserved his manipulation then. And Daniel didn't deserve his manipulation now. Neither did his other children or his grandchildren.

"I don't consider myself God," said Patrick.

Her tone was bitter. "Then why do you act like it?"

He stood up. "I believe this meeting is over."

"I'm serious, Patrick." She couldn't let it go. She knew deep down inside that this was her one and only chance to save Daniel, maybe to save Cullen and Bryan. "You have to stop."

His brow furrowed. "Stop what?"

"Holding on to your family with an iron fist."

"I guess you haven't heard. I'm stepping down as CEO."

She gave a scoffing laugh. "While making them pawns in your emotional chess game."

"Is that what you think I'm doing?"

"Isn't it?"

They stared at each other in silence for a moment.

"With all due respect, Amanda, I don't have to explain myself to you."

"You're right. You don't. But you'll eventually have to explain yourself to Daniel." Amanda shook her head. "One day he'll wake up. One day he'll see you for what you are."

"I think that day was today."

"Then you see my point."

Patrick considered her for a long moment. "No. But I think I see something else."

She waited.

"I think I see what you are to Daniel."

Amanda drew back. "What?" Did he know about their affair?

Patrick ran his knuckles along the back of her guest chair. "It seems my mistake wasn't in making you marry him. My mistake was in letting you divorce him."

"Letting me—"

"He still needs you, Amanda." Patrick gave a calculating smile, and it was even more frightening than his frown.

"Back off, Patrick."

"No, Amanda, I don't believe I will. Good day."

Twelve

Daniel figured it would take at least one lap around Central Park to work up his courage. And it might take another lap to convince Amanda they had a chance.

He pocketed the three carat diamond ring and double-checked the champagne he'd stashed under the seat of the carriage.

Julie had been a willing accomplice in getting Amanda to the park entrance at the right time. He didn't know what methods she'd used, but he could already see the two women walking up Sixty-Seventh Street.

He adjusted his tie, patted the square bulge in his breast pocket and started toward them along the crowded sidewalk.

"Amanda," he greeted.

"Daniel?"

"Gotta go," said Julie, quickly melting away.

Amanda spun toward the sound of Julie's voice. "What—"

"She must have had something to do," said Daniel, taking Amanda's arm and steering her around a cluster of tourists.

Amanda skipped a step, coming into pace with him, craning her neck. "She wanted me to look at a pair of shoes."

"Maybe she changed her mind." He slid his hand down to grasp hers.

Amanda blinked up at him dubiously. "Where did you come from?"

He jabbed over his shoulder with his thumb. "The park."

"Were you out walking?"

Daniel nodded. That seemed like as good a story as any.

He smiled down at her, and lowered his voice, ignoring the crowds parting around them.

"I missed you," he said, squeezing her hand.

Her expression relaxed, and her mocha eyes glinted with mischief. "I could stop by the office again."

He moved in closer. "I'll buy another tie."

She grinned, and he grinned right back, feeling giddy as a kid on Christmas morning.

She'd agree to marry him.

She *had* to agree to marry him.

Then they could make love every night, wake up together every morning, visit their grandchildren and grow old together. He lifted her hand and kissed her knuckles.

Daniel suddenly wanted nothing more than to grow old with Amanda.

Well, there was one other thing. But they could talk about that after he convinced her to marry him. He had a feeling she'd be in support of his career move.

"Or you could come to my office." She pulled their clasped hands toward her lips and kissed him back. "I've had this fantasy…"

"Oh, I like the sound of that."

Her expression turned slumberous.

"For now," he said, drawing back, forcing himself to concentrate on the proposal instead of future lovemaking, "I have a little fantasy of my own."

"Is it sexual?"

"Better than that. It's spontaneous."

She quirked an eyebrow.

"Come on." He tugged her through pedestrian traffic and into the park.

He stopped next to the reserved carriage.

"Hop in," he said to Amanda.

"*This* is your fantasy?"

"You're going to get picky on me?"

She shook her head. "No. No, of course not."

"Then hop in." He offered her a hand up.

She put one foot on the running board and stepped into the carriage.

He followed her up, closed the half door and signaled to the driver to start.

The horse's hooves clip-clopped on the pavement. Dusk was falling over the city, and skyscraper lights began to illuminate the skies. The trees around Tavern on the Green lit up as they passed.

Daniel stretched his arm across the back of the seat.

"It's beautiful at night," said Amanda.

He wrapped his arm around her shoulder. "You're what's beautiful out here."

"Yeah, yeah. You use that line often?"

"Nope."

She scoffed in disbelief.

"Hey, how often do you think I take women riding through the park?"

She turned to look at him. "I don't know. How often?"

"Rarely."

"But you have done it before."

"You're saying spontaneity only counts if it's a brand-new activity?"

"No. But you get bonus points for a brand-new activity."

"I wish you'd told me that earlier."

She laughed and leaned her head on his shoulder.

He felt her chest rise and fall as she breathed. Suddenly, his world felt perfect.

He kissed the top of her head and took her hand in his across their laps.

The sounds of the city faded, and the horse's hooves, the squeak of the carriage and the jangle of the harness brass filled the night.

He wanted to ask her the question, but first he wanted the ride to last forever.

"Champagne?" he muttered against her hair.

She sat up straighter. "Where are we going to get champagne."

He gave her an eyebrow waggle, pushed aside the lap robe and revealed the cooler. He popped the lid and pulled out a bottle of Laurent-Perrier along with two fluted glasses.

"Spontaneous?" she asked with a raised brow.

"I only thought of it this morning."

She shook her head, but her smile was beautiful.

He couldn't resist kissing her sweet mouth.

She wrapped her arms around his neck, eagerly participating.

"Who needs champagne?" he muttered, drawing her close and delving into the recesses of her mouth.

She pulled back and glanced pointedly at the champagne bottle. "Wouldn't want to screw up your carefully planned spontaneity."

He reached for it. "As long as you promise we can kiss later."

"We'll see."

"Would it kill you to plan *something*?"

"I like to keep my options open."

He handed her the glasses and then twisted the wire holder off the cork.

"I want you to consider me an option," he said, and popped the cork out with his thumbs.

The champagne bubbled out the top of the bottle, and Amanda laughed.

"An option tonight," said Daniel as he poured the effervescent liquid into the glasses. "And an option every night."

Her mouth pursed in confusion.

"Amanda," he breathed, wondering if he should drop to one knee. That would be the proper thing to do. But Amanda didn't have too high an opinion of doing the proper thing.

"Yes?" she prompted.

"These past few weeks...together." He took a breath. "They've meant a lot to me."

Her lips curved in a shy smile. "They've meant a lot to me, too," she said.

"I've remembered things." He glanced off into the dark trees and the city lights beyond. "I've felt things that I haven't felt in years."

He looked back into her eyes. "I've realized that my feelings for you were buried, but they hadn't changed."

"Daniel—"

He put a finger over her lips. "Shh."

He slowly drew his hand back and reached into his inside suit pocket. Retrieving the ring, he flipped the velvet case open with his thumb.

"Marry me, Amanda."

Her eyes went wide, and she sucked in a tight breath.

He rushed on before she had time to react. "I love you very much. I've never stopped loving you. I haven't been living these past fifteen years, just existing."

Her gaze shot from the ring to his face and back again.

"This is—"

"I know you think it's sudden. But we've known each other so well and for so long—"

"I was going to say, unbelievable." The tone of her voice wasn't quite right. It was flat, almost accusatory.

"Amanda?"

"He couldn't work this fast. Nobody works this fast."

Daniel stared at her. To be fair, it had been a few weeks. And they weren't exactly strangers. And they'd made love twice.

"I've given this a lot of thought."

"Have you? *Have* you?"

He flipped the conversation over in his mind, trying to figure out where it had gone off the rails. "Yeah."

She glanced at her watch. "He only left my office two hours ago."

"Who?"

She shook her head and laughed coldly. "No, Daniel. I won't marry you."

Her answer was like a stake in his heart.

"I won't be your family's pawn," she said.

Panic invaded his system as he scrambled for a way to change her mind. "How'd my family get into this?"

She dumped her champagne over the side. "Your family's been into it from the very start."

He stared at the empty glass. So that was it. He wasn't worth it.

"You're saying our love won't trump your aversion to my family?"

She dropped the empty glass into the cooler. "I'm saying take me home."

He snapped the case shut. "Right."

All night long, Amanda assured herself she'd made the right decision. Daniel didn't want to marry her. He didn't want to marry her any more than he wanted to be CEO of Elliott Publication Holdings.

Patrick had them all brainwashed, and there was nothing she could do to change that. The best she could do was save herself.

She'd definitely made the right decision.

And when her alarm clock went off, she was still telling herself just that.

She kept saying it all through her shower.

But over granola and tea she started asking questions. Scary, insidious questions.

Had she made the right decision?

Sure, Patrick was behind it, and Daniel might not have proposed again without his father's urging. But there was something there. There was magic between them. And she could have spent the rest of her life exploring it.

She dropped her granola spoon and buried her face in her hands. What if she'd made the biggest mistake of her life?

That had been one perfect ring.

It had been one perfect proposal.

And Daniel was one perfect guy.

Her arms suddenly felt empty. Ridiculous, considering she'd spent sixteen years without him and only a few weeks in his company again.

She was losing it here.

She had to get him out of her brain.

She picked up the telephone, automatically dialing Karen's number.

Olive put her right through.

"Hello?" came Karen's voice, cheerful despite the early hour.

"Karen? It's Amanda."

"Oh my God," Karen burst out. "Michael told me what happened."

"He did?"

"The whole family is talking about it."

Amanda sat back in her chair. "They are?"

"Of course they are. We can't believe it."

Amanda wasn't sure she was getting this right. Daniel had put his marriage proposal out there on the Elliott grapevine?

Unbelievable.

"Cullen overheard," said Karen. "And he called Bryan—"

"Cullen overheard what?"

Karen whistled low. "Patrick must be just fuming."

"Because I said no?"

There was a silent pause. "Because none of his children have ever dared yell at him before."

"I didn't—"

"I'd have paid money to see it. Michael said Daniel went up one side of him and down the other. Now they're all placing bets on who'll blink first."

"What do you mean who'll blink?" If they fought, they'd already made up. Because Patrick had apologized. And then he'd told Daniel to marry Amanda.

"They're no longer speaking to each other."

"No. That can't be right. They talked yesterday." In the afternoon. After Patrick had seen her. After Patrick had decided to make Daniel propose.

"No they didn't," said Karen. "Definitely not."

Amanda raked her fingers into her damp hair. This didn't make sense. Unless... Her eyes went wide. *Oh, no.*

"Amanda?" Karen's voice seemed to come from a long way off.

"I have to go."

"What—"

"I'll call you later." Amanda quickly hung up the phone. Something was seriously wrong. If Daniel hadn't talked to Patrick, then he'd proposed all on his own. But that couldn't be. Because that would mean...

Amanda swore out loud.

Daniel dropped the neatly typed letter on the top of his desk. He'd pictured Amanda here for this, pictured her smiling with pride, hanging on to his arm, making plans for a simple wedding—maybe on a boat off Madagascar.

He was ready to give her everything she wanted, everything she'd made him want. But she hadn't even let him make his case last night. She hadn't even listened to his plan, she'd simply written him off along with the rest of his family.

As if Daniel didn't have a life of his own. Sure, he liked to keep his family happy. It was usually easier to go with the tide than to fight it.

Truth was, he hadn't really cared a whole lot since Amanda had left him the first time.

But he'd come back to life.

She'd brought him back to life.

He was about to do every damn thing she'd ever asked of him, and she wouldn't even give him the courtesy of a fair hearing.

He plucked a gold pen from the holder on his desk and signed the letter of resignation with a flourish. Looked as though he was going to Madagascar alone.

His office door burst open.

He looked up, expecting Nancy, but Amanda rushed into the room.

She slowed her steps when she saw him, gazing quizzically, as if he'd sprouted horns.

Nancy quickly appeared behind her, clearly ready to escort Amanda back outside.

"It's fine," said Daniel, waving his secretary away.

Nancy nodded, pulling the door closed and leaving them alone.

"Something I can help you with?" he asked Amanda, focusing on the seascape behind her left ear. He wanted to cling to his anger, not take a good look at everything he was losing.

"I…uh…" She took another tentative step toward him. She cleared her throat. "I wanted…"

He plunked the pen back in its holder, not bothering to disguise his impatience. It was proving quite easy to hold on to his anger.

He crossed his arms over his chest, feeling strong enough to look into her dark eyes. "I'm a little busy this morning."

Her eyes were wide, liquid and strangely vulnerable, but he steeled himself against them.

She swallowed. "Why, Daniel?"

"Why what?"

She was silent for several heartbeats. "Why did you ask me to marry you?"

"I thought I made that pretty clear."

"I thought your father had talked to you."

"He talks to me all the time."

"Did he tell you to marry me?"

"Not since the seventies."

Her tone turned pleading. "Then, why?"

He shrugged. "Oh, I don't know. Since I have no brain of my own, I called one-nine-hundred, proper behavior, and they told me I should propose after the fifth—"

"Daniel."

"—date. They also suggested a carriage ride and champagne. Shipped me the ring, and gave me a wallet card full of catch phrases. You want to see it?"

"Daniel, stop."

He sighed. "I've got a big day coming up. Can you say whatever it is you came to say and get out?"

She recoiled from his anger.

Too bad. He wasn't feeling particularly charitable at the

moment. Especially not with her standing there looking so sexy and desirable, reminding him of what might have been.

"You're glaring at me," she accused.

"No, I'm not."

"Yes, you are. I can't say what I want to say with you glaring."

He let his arms drop to his sides and tried to soften his expression. Now he just wanted to get this over with. "Fine."

"I came to say I'm sorry." She moved in a little closer. "I also came to say…" She raked her teeth over her bottom lip. "That was one perfect ring."

His body went still, and her scent swirled out to tease him. She gently touched his arm, making him flinch.

"I'm sorry I misunderstood," she said. "But after your father—"

"My father?"

"He stopped at my office yesterday to apologize."

Daniel all but staggered against his desk. "My father *apologized* to you?"

"He said you told him to."

"Yeah, well…" Daniel nodded. "I did." But he never thought his father would do it. Not in a million years.

"Then he told me you still needed me. And then you showed up with a ring, and I—"

"Put two and two together?"

"And came up with seven. I'm so sorry, Daniel." Her hand trembled on his arm and she gazed into his eyes. "I really loved that ring."

A weight lifted from his shoulders. His chest tightened and his heart thudded deeply. "You saying you want it back?" He'd already returned it, but he could fix that with one phone call.

"It was perfect," she said.

"You hate perfect."

"Yeah? Well, I'm working on that." She slipped her arms

around his waist and settled her body against his. "Because you're perfect, and I really, really want you."

"I don't have the ring," he confessed.

Her eyes mirrored her disappointment.

He felt like a cad. He should have been prepared for this. He usually had contingency plans for his contingency plans.

Then his gaze caught the paper clip holding his letter of resignation.

On the other hand, he could try for spontaneity. He slipped the paper clip off and twisted it into a loop.

He held the makeshift ring out to Amanda. "But will you marry me anyway?"

She grinned and presented her finger, giving him an eager nod. "Yes. But don't think this gets you out of a big diamond and a well-planned proposal," she said.

He slipped the paper clip over her finger. "You hate it when I plan."

"I was thinking a suite at the Riverside. A few dozen roses. Champagne. A string quartet."

"Think I'll leave that one to you." He reached behind him and lifted the letter from the desktop, holding it in front of her eyes. "Because I have other plans to make."

"What's—" She adjusted the focal length and started to read. "I don't understand?"

"I'm offering Cullen my job as editor in chief."

She stared up at him. "Why?"

"I'm going traveling."

"Where?"

"Everywhere. I'll be looking into a new adventure magazine."

Her eyes went very wide. "Your father agreed?"

He shrugged his shoulders. "I don't know."

"You haven't asked him?"

"It was a spontaneous decision. You want to come along?"

A grin grew wide across her beautiful face. "You bet."

Amanda smiled to herself as she snuggled up to Daniel's bare chest.

Cullen had accepted the position of editor in chief of *Snap*, and Patrick had agreed amazingly easily to let Daniel investigate an adventure magazine for Elliott Publications. Bryan and Cullen were ecstatic about the reunion and made their parents promise to get married before they left on their travels.

They had no plans so far, but Amanda wasn't worried. Sooner or later, Daniel would give in to temptation and rent a ballroom somewhere.

She kissed his chest. "Have I mentioned lately that I love you?"

Daniel kissed the top of her head and gave her a squeeze. "Not for about thirty minutes. But that yodel thing you did was good for my ego."

She elbowed him. "I did *not* yodel."

"Sure, you did."

"Are you going to keep making stuff up?"

"Yeah."

Then he stroked her hair with his wide palm. "No more planning. From now on, I'm making stuff up as I go along."

Her chest tightened. "I don't want you to change for me."

"I'm changing for me. And partly for you, because you're the best thing I never planned. I love you, Amanda," he whispered gruffly and drew her into his arms.

The phone beside his bed interrupted their kiss.

Amanda checked the clock. "Who on earth—"

Daniel picked up the phone. "Hello? Cullen?"

Amanda sat straight up.

"Is she okay?" Then Daniel grinned. "Are *they* okay?"

They?

Daniel covered the mouthpiece. "It's a girl."

Amanda jumped out of bed and grabbed for her clothes.

"Seven pounds, six ounces," said Daniel. "Maeve Amanda Elliott."

Amanda's chest contracted and her eyes filled with tears.

"Come on," she whispered to Daniel.

"We're on our way," he laughed into the phone.

"We're grandparents," said Amanda as she climbed into her slacks.

They made it to the hospital in less than fifteen minutes.

While they stood at the nursery window, scanning name tags, trying to locate their new granddaughter, a harried Cullen burst through the swinging doors of the maternity wing.

"Mom," he cried, his yellow paper gown flapping around the knees of his pants. He immediately pulled Amanda into a tight embrace. She had to gasp for breath as he rocked her back and forth.

He kissed the top of her head, his strong voice cracking. "I can't believe what you went through for me. How can I ever thank you?"

Amanda's chest swelled, and she blinked back a sheen of tears. "You don't have to thank me," she whispered against his chest. "You were the most wonderful son in the world."

Cullen pulled back to look into her eyes. "Oh, Mom."

She grinned at him, smoothing back his damp hair from his forehead. "Congratulations, Dad."

He shook his head in disbelief.

Then he turned to Daniel and held out his hand. "And, Dad. You did this. You did this twice!"

Daniel chuckled, shaking Cullen's hand and pulling his son into an embrace.

Amanda wiped away the tears as they spilled over her lashes.

Cullen turned to gaze through the nursery glass to where

a nurse was wheeling in a bassinet. "There she is," he sighed. "Oh, she's so tiny."

"She's supposed to be tiny," said Daniel.

Amanda moved up to the window while the nurse placed the bassinet in the center of the front row, giving them a warm smile.

"I'm almost afraid to touch her," Cullen confessed.

Daniel patted him on the back. "You'll be fine, son. You'll feed her, change her and bathe her, and before you know it, she'll be begging you for bedtime stories."

Cullen gave a forced chuckle and put an arm around each of his parents. "I just hope I make it through the first twenty-four hours."

Amanda leaned her head against her son. "She's beautiful."

"She is," he agreed.

"How's Misty?" asked Daniel.

Cullen blinked rapidly. "She's perfect. She's wonderful." He drew a breath. "She's sleeping now."

"Hey, bro. Way to go!" Bryan and Lucy arrived and the three separated so Cullen could greet his brother.

Daniel shifted closer to Amanda as the Elliott family began streaming into the nursery hallway. She felt the familiar stirrings of unease as first five, then nine, then twelve of them crowded around the window, talking and joking with each other.

By the time Patrick and Maeve rounded the corner, Amanda's stomach was cramping with insecurity. What had she gotten herself into?

"It's going to be okay," Daniel whispered into her hair, sliding an arm around her waist.

But Amanda wasn't so sure.

Then Patrick gave her a nod and a smile of greeting. Karen called her name and sent her a wave across the crowd. And Daniel pulled her tight into the circle of his strong arms.

Little Maeve opened her mouth in a wide yawn, and there was a collective sigh from the assembled adults. It was obvious their hearts had melted then and there for the newest Elliott.

Amanda leaned her head against Daniel's chest and drew hope from the enduring bonds of his family. There might be bumps on the road ahead, but they were going to make it this time.

Together.

* * * * *

Don't miss the next installment
of THE ELLIOTS.
Pick up THE INTERN AFFAIR
by Roxanne St.Clair,
available in August
from Silhouette Desire.

The next book in
THE BRIDES OF BELLA LUCIA *series*
is out next month!
Don't miss THE REBEL PRINCE
by Raye Morgan
Here's an exclusive sneak preview
of Emma Valentine's story!

"OH, NO!"

The reaction slipped out before Emma Valentine could stop it, for there stood the very man she most wanted to avoid seeing again.

He didn't look any happier to see her.

"Well, come on, get on board," he said gruffly. "I won't bite." One eyebrow rose. "Though I might nibble a little," he added, mostly to amuse himself.

But she wasn't paying any attention to what he was saying. She was staring at him, taking in the royal-blue uniform he was wearing, with gold braid and glistening badges decorating the sleeves, epaulettes and an upright collar. Ribbons and medals covered the breast of the short, fitted jacket. A gold-encrusted sabre hung at his side. And suddenly it was clear to her who this man really was.

She gulped wordlessly. Reaching out, he took her elbow and pulled her aboard. The doors slid closed. And finally she found her tongue.

"You...you're the prince."

He nodded, barely glancing at her. "Yes. Of course."

She raised a hand and covered her mouth for a moment. "I should have known."

"Of course you should have. I don't know why you didn't." He punched the ground-floor button to get the elevator moving again, then turned to look down at her. "A relatively bright five-year-old child would have tumbled to the truth right away."

Her shock faded as her indignation at his tone asserted itself. He might be the prince, but he was still just as annoying as he had been earlier that day.

"A relatively bright five-year-old child without a bump on the head from a badly thrown water polo ball, maybe," she said defensively. She wasn't feeling woozy any longer and she wasn't about to let him bully her, no matter how royal he was. "I was unconscious half the time."

"And just clueless the other half, I guess," he said, looking bemused.

The arrogance of the man was really galling.

"I suppose you think your 'royalness' is so obvious it sort of shimmers around you for all to see?" she challenged. "Or better yet, oozes from your pores like…like sweat on a hot day?"

"Something like that," he acknowledged calmly. "Most people tumble to it pretty quickly. In fact, it's hard to hide even when I want to avoid dealing with it."

"Poor baby," she said, still resenting his manner. "I guess that works better with injured people who are half asleep." Looking at him, she felt a strange emotion she couldn't identify. It was as though she wanted to prove something to him, but she wasn't sure what. "And anyway, you know you did your best to fool me," she added.

His brows knit together as though he really didn't know what she was talking about. "I didn't do a thing."

"You told me your name was Monty."

"It is." He shrugged. "I have a lot of names. Some of them

are too rude to be spoken to my face, I'm sure." He glanced at her sideways, his hand on the hilt of his sabre. "Perhaps you're contemplating one of those right now."

You bet I am.

That was what she would like to say. But it suddenly occurred to her that she was supposed to be working for this man. If she wanted to keep the job of coronation chef, maybe she'd better keep her opinions to herself. So she clamped her mouth shut, took a deep breath and looked away, trying hard to calm down.

The elevator ground to a halt and the doors slid open laboriously. She moved to step forward, hoping to make her escape, but his hand shot out again and caught her elbow.

"Wait a minute. *You're* a woman," he said, as though that thought had just presented itself to him.

"That's a rare ability for insight you have there, Your Highness," she snapped before she could stop herself. And then she winced. She was going to have to do better than that if she was going to keep this relationship on an even keel.

But he was ignoring her dig. Nodding, he stared at her with a speculative gleam in his golden eyes. "I've been looking for a woman, but you'll do."

She blanched, stiffening. "I'll do for what?"

He made a head gesture in a direction she knew was opposite of where she was going and his grip tightened on her elbow.

"Come with me," he said abruptly, making it an order.

She dug in her heels, thinking fast. She didn't much like orders. "Wait! I can't. I have to get to the kitchen."

"Not yet. I need you."

"You what?" Her breathless gasp of surprise was soft, but she knew he'd heard it.

"I need you," he said firmly. "Oh, don't look so shocked. I'm not planning to throw you into the hay and have my way with you. I need you for something a bit more mundane than that."

She felt color rushing into her cheeks and she silently begged it to stop. Here she was, formless and stodgy in her chef's whites. No makeup, no stiletto heels. Hardly the picture of the femmes fatales he was undoubtedly used to. The likelihood that he would have any carnal interest in her was remote at best. To have him think she was hysterically defending her virtue was humiliating.

"Well, what if I don't want to go with you?" she said in hopes of deflecting his attention from her blush.

"Too bad."

"What?"

Amusement sparkled in his eyes. He was certainly enjoying this. And that only made her more determined to resist him.

"I'm the prince, remember? And we're in the castle. My orders take precedence. It's that old pesky divine rights thing."

Her jaw jutted out. Despite her embarrassment, she couldn't let that pass.

"Over my free will? Never!"

Exasperation filled his face.

"Hey, call out the historians. Someone will write a book about you and your courageous principles." His eyes glittered sardonically. "But in the meantime, Emma Valentine, you're coming with me."

ANGELS OF THE BIG SKY
by Roz Denny Fox

(#1368)

Widow Marlee Stein returns to Montana with her
young daughter, ready to help out with Cloud Chasers,
the flying service owned by her brother. When Marlee
takes over piloting duties, she finds herself in conflict
with a client, ranger Wylie Ames. Too bad Marlee's
attracted to a man she doesn't even want to like!

On sale September 2006!

THE CLOUD CHASERS—
Life is looking up.

Watch for the second story in Roz Denny Fox's two-
book series THE CLOUD CHASERS, available in
December 2006.

*Available wherever books are sold, including most
bookstores, supermarkets, discount stores and drugstores.*

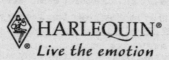

HARLEQUIN®
Live the emotion